"I'm besotted with this beguiling, hilarious, rollocking, language-metamorphosing novel. The future of the queer avant-garde is safe with Isabel Waidner."
Olivia Laing

Gaudy Bauble

Isabel Waidner

Dostoyevsky Wannabe Originals
An Imprint of Dostoyevsky Wannabe

First Published in 2017
by Dostoyevsky Wannabe Originals

Dostoyevsky Wannabe Originals is an imprint of Dostoyevsky Wannabe publishing.

Cover Design by Victoria Brown, based on an image by Isabel Waidner.

dostoyevskywannabe.com

ISBN-13: 978-1999924522
ISBN-10: 1999924525

"The actors are not all 'us'."
Donna Haraway, *The Promises of Monsters*, 1992

"Camp coup or butch putsch?"
Gaudy Bauble

"One cannot, however, safely invent an angel."
Jack Spicer, *The Unvert Manifesto*, 1954

For Lisa Blackman (Blulip).

TULEP

A formidable micro-horse sprang across a Formica tabletop. Ah, it's Tulep. Tulep sprang across grassgreen Formica, grazing, apparently. Besides, a white plastic laptop stood on the tabletop. Someone was maltreating its keyboard, trailblazing, apparently. Trailblazer Belà Gotterbarm was wearing a chequered *Beirendonck* skirt, worse-for-wear trainers and tennis socks. She was wearing her soft-cotton Pegasus print sweater. The Pegasus on Belà's sweater reared and raised her wings. Pink flashes and green graffiti on extra soft cotton manifested Pegasus energy. On the other hand, Tulep was posturing atop the Formica tabletop like a formidable female stallion. Quite like the Pegasus on Belà's sweater was a winged horse, Tulep was a budgerigar with atypical hooves. Heh, Peggy! Tulep, heh. Raised pinions, Tulep was pawing Formica. Was this territorial posturing? A mutual 'Piss Off'? Or a macho stand-off? Heh, Pegface! Tuleper, heh. But this was not a territorial stand-off. This was not *Highlander* (1986), the British fantasy action film. This was a get-together of disenfranchised things. This was a faggoty social. A working class knees-up. A cocky conspiracy? From Hoofed Winged Thing to Hoofed Winged Thing. From one Hoofed Winged Thing to another. From mythological chimera to genetic chimerism. Peggy <3 Tulep. And Tulep <3 Peggy. They were giving each other ideas. And this was just the beginning.

Belà Gotterbarm wrote awkwardgarde fiction, potentially trailblazing. In a 10th floor council flat on Harpur Street, central London, Belà's white plastic laptop stood atop the Formica tabletop. Unaware of the faggoty social taking place under her nose, Belà was working on the script for a new 8-part television series, working title Querbird. According to director/producer Tracey B. Lulip, filming was due to get underway ASAP, preferably yesterday. Belà had promised a tone-and-*milieu*-setting, intrigue-inciting pilot by tomorrow afternoon.

In terms of the writing process, Belà's pet bird and the tabletop's hound's-tooth pattern proved influential, rather than Peggy the Pegasus, say. Confronting the bird/hound's-tooth conundrum that faced her head-on, Belà invented a generic canary character. To Belà's mind, the canary was the optimal birdhound, or birddog. (Etymologically, 'canary' derives from Latin *canis*, genitive: *canarius*; which in return relates to the English word 'canine'.) Belà typed the word 'Canary'. Good. Querbird began like this: 'Canary'. Canaries as a species originate from the Canary Islands, or *Insula Canaria*, literally 'Island of Dogs', so called because large dogs lived there. On the other hand, Tulep originated not from the Island of Dogs, but the Isle of Dogs in the East End of London. This, however, did not make Tulep a natural birddog. There was an excess of filly in her. A filly is a female foal. Also etymologically, the 'Dog' in the Isle of Dogs appears to be a corruption of a precedent 'Duck', as in the Isle of Ducks, or 'Dyke', as in the Isle of Super-Dykes. Tulep had dyke written all over her. Above filly, Tulep had dyke written all over her.

Belà's second draft replaced the Canary, the optimal birddog, with of all things a budgerigar. Deleting 'Canary', Belà typed 'Hoofed Budgerigar'. What? Why?! Tulep was not the optimal birddog! But this was the Pegasus off Belà's sweater putting her foot down. This was Peggy the Pegasus throwing her weight behind Tulep. From Hoofed Winged Thing to Hoofed Winged Thing. From one Hoofed Winged Thing to another. This was the recently formed H.W.T. (Hoofed Winged Things) alliance exerting its influence. This was the H.W.T. alliance winging its way into the Querbird script. Was this a camp coup? A butch putsch? An attack on generic things? Mobilising knees-up resources, Peggy was as if electrified. Pink flashes surrounded her head. Green graffiti. Peggy was so energetic. Peggy embodied H.W.T. solidarity, and a let's-go mentality. An appetite to get going. The phrase *'On y va!'* ran towards the hem of Belà's sweater in metallic lettering. Peggy was the bye-bye-saying, never-to-be-seen-again type of migrant

Pegasus. This was Peggy, the let's-get-the-hell-out-of-here Pegasus. This was *Aufnimmerwiedersehen* Peggy. Peggy was raring to go and she was taking no prisoners. On her way out, Peggy walked all over the Querbird Canary. Peggy walked all over the generic Canary, paving the way for her Hoofed Winged Kin, Tulep.

This was bad news for the Querbird script. Bad news all round. After a promising start, Querbird was real-time derailing. Bye bye, generic Canary. Bye bye, optimal birddog. Belà Gotterbarm's second draft read like this:

'Querbird Pilot (Gotterbarm, 201x)

Hoofed Budgerigar Of The Isle Of Dogs.
Hoofed Budgerigar Off To Canary Wharf.
? Goes To The Dogs.'

When Belà looked up from her laptop, Tulep was gone. Tulep?! Tulep! The window stood slightly ajar. Bird corrupted by flighty Pegasus? 'Hoofed Budgerigar Off To The Isle Of Dogs'? Off to the Isle of Super-Dykes, an imagined stronghold. An imagined Fire Island in the East End of London. An insular Old Compton Street, or Hebden-Bridge-by-the-Thames. Aborting Querbird, Belà Gotterbarm undertook a significant costume change and went after Tulep. This was not quite a camp coup, nor a butch putsch. But it was a beginning.

TRACEY BIRYUKOV LULIP

Tracey Biryukov Lulip lived in a 320 sq ft 10th floor council flat on Harpur Street, WC1N. Tracey had lived here since 1991. Tracey B. Lulip, she went by the name of Blulip. Blulip had stuck. The bell went. Blulip opened the door. Oh, hello! It was P.I. Belahg. Hello hello! From the beginning Tracey B. Lulip and P.I. Belahg resembled each other in a Gilbert & George kind of way. They were not quite the lesbian Gilbert Prousch (1943-) and George Passmore (1942-). They were not quite 'Singing and Living Sculptures'. Their heads were not covered in multi-coloured, metallised powders, nor did they wear matching suits. Yet they resembled each other in a distinctly Gilbert & George kind of way.

Blulip was wearing her azure-blue, white-mini-star T-shirt and her camouflage joggers from *Tesco*. P.I. Belahg was wearing her *Comme Des Garçons* shirt with Mexican-inspired pompom detailing fringing the button tab and the chest pocket and *Y-3 Hero* joggers. Both P.I. Belahg and Blulip were wearing worse-for-wear *adidas* trainers and tennis socks. Blulip presented the P.I. with a foot high crudely carved object that looked like an idol, a deity, or a bludgeon. Belahg, look. On closer inspection, the object was a primitive model of a budgerigar, generously blue and white lacquered, with a crimson, a bloodstained? mouth? Healthy-lips, Blulip asserted. This was Healthy-lips, apparently. According to Blulip, Healthy-lips was the female lead of the forthcoming Querbird TV series. "Can I borrow a biro?" P.I. Belahg interjected. P.I. Belahg wrote 'Healthy-lips = female lead' on the back of her hand. Healthy-lips was Blulip's only reliable asset, apparently. I'll explain, Blulip said. Come into my workshop.

Workshop was another word for Blulip's 200 sq ft living-room/kitchen. A workbench covered in tools, wood chips and paint tubes backed onto the wall to the left. Ahead, a basic kitchen unit. An electric oven. A mini-*Fridgette*. A series of budgerigar figurines lined up behind the sink like a biological development study. "Healthy-lips's stunt doubles," Blulip said. Amidst sketches, newspaper cut-outs, photos and postcards, a theatre backcloth depicting 'daylight' was gaffer-taped to the wall. "Nice view," Belahg said, looking out of the Critall window. "Tiny flat. And who are they? Blocking the sunlight?" "Who? Oh, they. Supporting cast," Blulip said.

A theatre backcloth depicting 'night' was mounted to a stand blocking most of the Critall window. Various fibreglass sculptures, all hoofed animals, stood in the foreground. "Yes, they," P.I. Belagh said. I mean?! Hoofed Bear, Hoofed Cub, Hoofed Otter, Hoofed Owl, Hoofed Gazelle, Hoofed Pussycat, Hoofed Marmoset, Hoofed Afghan and Hoofed Cygnet were the Querbird supporting cast, apparently. They appeared to be grazing in front of the one million mini-star backcloth (depicting 'night'). "Belahg, look." For demonstration purposes, Blulip entered the scenery. Her white-mini-star T-shirt was meant to blend in with the backcloth, apparently. "Belahg, see?" The T-shirt enabled her manually to animate the various ungulates without appearing on film. Blulip pulled a mini-star cap over her head. She manipulated Hoofed Otter. "Your joggers," Belahg said. "I hate to say." Blulip's joggers and the backcloth clashed, foiling her camouflage. Not that there was a camera on set. There was no discernible camera on set.

According to Blulip, this was the low budget production of Querbird, a new TV series for Channel 4. No, let me rephrase this. Blulip rephrased this. This was not the low budget production of Querbird. This was a travesty. This was the Querbird production real-time derailing. In Socialist Britain (here, now), public-service TV broadcaster Channel 4 routinely commissioned diverse producers. In Socialist Britain, Channel 4 were committed to innovative and representative programming 24/7. Most of Querbird's budget, however, had gone. Most of Channel 4's advance had gone to one Belà Gotterbarm, Querbird's appointed writer. "Belà Gotterbarm!" Belahg said. Who had not heard of Belà Gotterbarm? Awkwardgarde fiction pioneer. Agender feminist, transgender activist. P.I. Belahg, for one, was impressed. On the other hand, Blulip was unimpressed. Early on in the writing process, Belà's bird had run off, apparently. To Blulip-knew-not-where, Whitstable. Some lesbian *Hochburg*. Belà had gone after her bird. Not caring two hoots for Querbird, Belà had gone AWOL. Belà had aborted Querbird in its fledgling stages, landing her, Blulip, in it. What was Blulip to do without an adequate script, pluck something out of thin air? Make it up as she went along? Film first, story-board later? What about scenery, props, casting? What about a run-in period?

Alarmingly, Blulip had riffed on the script already. Rather than stall, Blulip had structured the pre-production process around Belà's Querbird fragment. "Based on this, I bought that." Based on lines such as 'Hoofed Bird Of The Isle Of Dogs' (Gotterbarm, 201x), Blulip had Google-searched 'Hoofed Bird', or 'Hoofed Budgerigar'. Something like that. An unknown, presumably hostile algorithm had shown results for 'hoofed cygnet' instead. 'Showing results for hoofed cygnet', Google had said. Hence Blulip had come across the Hoofed Cygnet probate sale. The Hoofed Cygnet had been a themed pub in the Portsmouth area (Boscombe?). Blulip could not remember the details. She'd gone blank. Blulip had purchased the Hoofed Cygnet probate on *eBay*, for cheap. So cheap, it had cost the seller to get rid.

Later, P.I. Belahg attempted to reproduce the result, searching a number of items, including 'hoofed animal' and 'Hoofed Budgerigar'. None of her searches produced links relating to the Hoofed Cygnet probate sale, nor the Hoofed Cygnet pub near Portsmouth. Taxidermy, yes. DEER HOOF COAT HOOK (free click and collect at Argos), yes. Yes yes, Equimins™ Hoof Disinfectant Trigger Spray, *Numero Uno* for equine thrush infections. But 'Hoofed Cygnet probate sale'? 'Hoofed Cygnet pub/bar/café' in Boscombe? No. Nothing. The Hoofed Cygnet probate sale had been a one-off result.

Shortly after the purchase, 9 life-size fibreglass sculptures had arrived at Blulip's on Harpur Street. Blulip had been having second thoughts ever since. Blulip had concerns that she should have gathered together half of the Querbird cast plus *on spec*. No mention of *them* in *this*. Belahg, have a read-through. Blulip picked up a single page print-out of Belà's Querbird manuscript. Have a read-through, why not. See for yourself. Blulip had concerns that most of her assets procured during pre-production should fail to appear in the original script. She had concerns that, to date, Healthy-lips should be the one *bona fide* Querbird on set. Even Healthy-lips's central status derived from a four-sentencer, literally. "Let's have a look." P.I. Belahg took the script. "'Hoofed Budgerigar Of The Isle Of Dogs'?! What do you mean, 'Hoofed Budgerigar Off To Canary Wharf'? Bird Dogs Dykes? Seriously? Anyway, no," the P.I. confirmed. No mention of Hoofed Marmoset. No Hoofed Pussycat. No mention of 'night', nor 'day'. P.I. Belahg agreed that Blulip's Querbird pre-production appeared to have veered off-*piste*. Blulip's TV series was departing from Belà's manuscript before filming had even started.

Blulip took her magic-white-mini-star-cap off, looking Belahg straight in the eye. "That's where you come in." Director/producer Tracey B. Lulip expected P.I. Belahg to come in at this point and relieve her predicament. Channel 4's cash could be lining P.I. Belahg's pockets, Blulip suggested. "P.I. Belahg?" "Yes?" "Find Belà Gotterbarm and her runaway bird. Will you? Help the Querbird production get back on track?" "Don't worry, Tracey," Belahg replied. Channel 4's cash would be cash well spent.

LOVEDAY

Blulip registered with interest that P.I. Belahg moved herself in for the purpose of the investigation. P.I. Belahg had moved herself into Blulip's 320 sq ft council flat in central London, WC1N. Already the Mexican-style pompom shirt hung over the back of the chair. Asked to elaborate on her strategy, P.I. Belahg declared that she objected to gungho operations, kneejerk manhunts, and heavy-handed detective work. Rollercoaster-frisking the Isle of Dogs, for example, was an operational no-go. P.I. Belahg preferred a methodological approach to forensics. At present, she was reluctant to push the investigation beyond certain conservative boundaries including the front door. Do consider the weather on the Isle of Dogs, Blulip. Have you heard of the British Summer? P.I. Belahg relaxed in her chair.

The bell went. Blulip opened the door. Hi. "Blue-Tit? P.I. Loveday, Holborn Detectives PLC." P.I. Loveday flashed a company ID card. Hi, really? Ok. P.I. Loveday was a rival investigator. P.I. Loveday and Tracey B. Lulip did not resemble each other in a Gilbert & George kind of way. There was nothing Gilbert-&-George-like about P.I. Loveday and Tracey B. Lulip. "Shall we discuss your case?" P.I. Loveday asked. "Ok," Blulip said, perhaps rather than 'who called you'? Blulip began to detail the events effecting Querbird's derailment. P.I. Loveday's digital Dictaphone was recording. In mid-sentence, P.I. Belahg chipped in. P.I. Belahg was hijacking Blulip's statement, providing her own professional take on the case. According to P.I. Belahg, the Hoofed Budgerigar of the Querbird script and her incarnations in wood were their strongest connections to Tulep, thence the bare bones of the inquiry. Healthy-lips constituted their primary investigative lead. Belahg showed Loveday the notation on the back of her hand. "It says 'female lead'," Loveday objected. Female lead, NOT investigative lead. P.I. Belahg did not flinch. "There's more," she continued. Red-lipper Healthy-lips was also a suspect, Belahg felt. The mouth on her. What you think, Loveday. From P.I. to P.I.. Let's have a look, shall we. Belahg fetched Healthy-lips. What's this, Belahg said, examining her investigative lead in front of P.I. Loveday. Ah, a suction cup. Evidently, a silicone sucker had been superglued to Heathy-lips's base. A make-shift hoof that facilitates flying. Like this. PHUT. P.I. Belahg got on a chair, suckering Healthy-lips to the ceiling. Loveday, look! Healthy-lips hung headfirst from the ceiling. P.I. Loveday paused her digi-Dictaphone. What, are you nuts?! P.I. Loveday from Holborn Detectives PLC dismissed P.I. Belahg outright, and her approach to forensics. P.I. Loveday preferred to speak to her client directly. "Blue-Tit," Loveday said to Blulip. "I am going to survey the bedroom." Oh. Ok. P.I. Loveday slipped on a pair of protective gloves and disposable overshoes. She excused herself. Nice view, she called from next door. P.I. Loveday took photographs to ensure that a permanent record existed of the site in the state in which it was found. She collected forensic evidence. She folded small, dry items in paper and sealed them in polythene bags. She sealed wet items in polythene bags for freezing, especially those containing potential biological samples. P.I. Loveday took notes and drew sketches. "Evidence 4.1.2. Grassgreen Formica/Hound's-tooth pattern: vvvvv. Evidence 4.2. White Plastic MacBook ©1983-2009, Mac OS X. Evidence 4.3.1. Soft-cotton sweater with Pegasus print & '*On Y Va!*' inscription. Evidence 5.0. Fingerprints on White Plastic Keyboard. Evidence 5.1. 1.5 cm diameter horseshoe footprints on hound's-tooth Formica.

Next door, Healthy-lips swooped from the ceiling. Healthy-lips nosedived and headbutted Blulip in the mouth. Whaaaat?! You ok? There was something the matter with Blulip's lip. You ok?! I'm... ohh-kehh. Mere scratch. Barely throbbing, look. But blood did not stop from coming. Also, a tooth had come loose. Oh dear. Now there were tears, too.

P.I. Loveday returned to the living-room/workshop

with her briefcase chocka. She sealed off the bedroom with three inch pink gaffer tape. "Blue-Tit," Loveday addressed Blulip. "Keep out. No trespassing." P.I. Loveday expressed concerns over the potential contamination of the relevant site. At Holborn Detectives PLC, they valued professionalism. "Blue-Tit," P.I. Loveday said. "Hm?" "What's with your face? Something wrong with your face." "Blulip, let's go," Belahg interrupted. "Now." In view of Blulip's bleeding from the mouth, Belahg insisted they visit A&E as a matter of urgency. "Ok," P.I. Loveday said. "I'll just wrap up in here. Leave me the keys, and I'll let myself out?" "No," P.I. Belahg objected. NO. No keys. Just shut the door behind you. Thank you. Good riddance. Then Belahg took Blulip to Guy's and St. Thomas's Dental Emergencies. Tower Wing, 21st floor. Nice view.

ORSUN URSOL

The breathless zoo were falling all over themselves, welcoming them back. In P.I. Belahg and Blulip's absence, several members of their fibreglass zoo appeared to have fallen over. Apart from the pink cordon sealing off the bedroom, there was no sign of P.I. Loveday. What a relief. Blulip had lost her Maxillary First Bicuspid (First Premolar), left upper 4. Also, Blulip had lost her Maxillary First Molar, left upper 6. Headbutted in the mouth by a nosediving budgerigar figurine. A propos, Belahg said, scanning the room. Where's Healthy-lips? No sign of Healthy-lips. But what's that?! Fluorescent green chalk had appeared on the linoleum floor. Fluorescent green chalk was outlining an unusually-shaped body on the workshop's linoleum floor. Neon-green, glow-in-the-dark, hi-vis speciality chalk was outlining a molar-shaped body on the workshop's linoleum floor. The molar-shaped body was surrounded by blood splatters. P.I. Belahg, for one, could not concentrate in this chaos. She could not function in this farrago. Blulip. Look at the state of it. Let's clear up. Help Hoofed Bear off the lino, for example. Help fallen Hoofed Cub stand up. Not to mention Hoofed Otter, Hoofed Owl, Hoofed Gazelle, Hoofed Afghan, Hoofed Cygnet, Hoofed Marmoset and Hoofed Pussycat. A cygnet is a baby swan. Is not detective work labelling work? Let's arrange these fibreglass animals in a meaningful order, like P.I. Loveday might. What we got. Bear, Cub, Otter, Owl, Gazelle, Afghan, Cygnet, Marmoset and Pussycat. BEAR CUB OTTER OWL GAZELLE AFGHAN CYGNET MARMOSET PUSSYCAT?! This animal sequence might not signify to most people. This animal sequence might mean nothing to most people, but it signalled in full Technicolour rainbows to P.I. Belahg. BCOOGACMP_OMG! "Blulip," Belahg said. "Hm?" "Where did you get these from, again?" Internet. Not *eBay*, admittedly. *gayBay.co.uk*. Historical interior décor of a rural gay dive. The Gay Cygnet. Or The Hoofed Cygnet, Blulip could not remember. Portsmouth area, I told you. The Gay or Hoofed Cygnet had been closed down in 1991 at the height of the AIDS crisis. The police had worn neoprene surgical gloves to protect against the HIV virus. Wet wipes, moist towelettes. Following the forced closure, The Gay Cygnet's décor had been stored away in the landlord's garden-shed. The Gay Cygnet's landlord had been Faglord Cygnet. Faglord Cygnet had preferred a feminine pronoun at all cost. Recently, The Gay Cygnet's décor had been auctioned off as part of Faglord Cygnet's late estate. She had had no immediate descendants.

The Gay Cygnet's hysterical décor embodied a 1980s taxonomy that in return emblematised Post-Village-People gay stereotypes. This taxonomy had been the invention of newspaper columnist George Mazzei, whose *Who's Who at the Zoo?* had been published in *The Advocate* (an "LGBT-interest magazine") on July 26, 1979. Effectively, *Who's Who at the Zoo?* had been a gay taxonomy, or as the original subtitle had had it, *A Glossary of Gay Animals*. The article had categorised homosexuals as Gay Bears, Owls, Cygnets, Pussycats, Gazelles, Afghans, and Marmosets. Predating for example *Bear Magazine*, which had not appeared until 1986, *Who's Who at the Zoo?* had arguably inaugurated the Gay Bear identity category. Cub and Otter were subdivisions of the prolific Gay Bear identity category that had not featured in the original *Who's Who*. Neither had Ursula featured in Mazzei's *Who's Who*. An Ursula was a lesbian-identified Bear, or a Bear-identified lesbian. Was it true that post-identity Britain did not know what a Bear was? A large, hairy, butch, gay man, with "notably muscular legs" (Mazzei, 1979). Or what a Cub was. A younger, large, hairy, butch, gay man. An Otter. A less large, less hairy, gay man, whose age was irrelevant. Ursula derived from Latin *ursus,* for bear. And/or it derived from the Disney character, octopus sorceress, and *The Little Mermaid*'s main antagonist, Ursula. Beyond baby swan, 'cygnet' might not signify to most people. According to Mazzei (1979), a Cygnet devoted his life to cultivating a perfect body and the sporting of *Gucci* loafers. Neoliberal Britain, however, was post that. Post-Cub, post-Otter, post-Ursula. Certainly post-Cygnet. Neoliberal Britain was post-identity before having learned the first thing about Cubs. Confounding post-identity Britain, gay taxa took centre stage in Blulip's council flat/workshop. Gay taxa experienced *einen zweiten Frühling* (a second spring). Flummoxing, consternating, insulting, disturbing and haunting post-identity Britain, lazarus taxa, things rampant, were outstaying their welcome. Historical gay identities had taken control of the workshop! Also The King's Arms on Old Compton Street. And The Duke of Wellington on Wardour Street. The Royal Vauxhall Tavern (RVT). And *Horse Meat Disco* at the manly Eagle on Kennington Lane. Bear culture was thriving in post-identity Britain. And the Bears were recruiting. Historical fictions were alive in Blulip's D.I.Y. workshop and studio, and also The King's Arms on Old Compton.

"It's attitude that makes a Bear." (Mazzei, 1979)

In P.I. Belahg's view, the Male Owl should have been in a museum. The Male Owl should have been in the V&A. The Male Owl had lived, fought, and died for today's QUILTBAG communities (Queer, Undecided, Intersex, Lesbian, Trans, Bi-sexual, Asexual, Gay). Male Owl had kept camp alive in the face of adversity. Male Owl had kept herself alive at a personal cost. Post-identity Britain however was post that, and the V&A had not bid at The Gay Cygnet *gayBay* auction. The Gay Cygnet bargain sale. Post-identity Britain prefers to forget and get over both, the Male Owl and the gay past. To Belahg, the Male Owl had become an inspiration again. Long live the Male Owl. On the other hand, Blulip was not so sure. On the other hand, Blulip was positively fed up with the Male Owl.

Blulip's fibreglass taxa were hooved. A horse's foot is a horse's foot is a horse's foot. Everything was equipped with a *Pferdefuss* (horse's foot). A *Pferdefuss* is a jinx or a drawback. *Pferdefüsse* wherever you looked. *Pferdefüsse* galore at Blulip's on Harpur Street. The *Pferdefüsse* signified longstanding PROBLEMS with Gay Bears, Cubs, and significant Otters.

The stereotyping. Any inter/trans identiy categories, anywhere? Maybe/maybe not. Intersectionality? Race? Class? At the very least lesbians had been included in the *Who's Who*, as a sort of afterthought. They had been mainly Owls, maybe Cygnets. As far as "gay women" (Mazzei, 1979) were concerned, none of the categories had really caught on. Ursula did not redress the derivative status of lesbians in Massey's Gay Zoo. Is the derivative status of lesbians behind the unquestioned absence of the womanly Eagle on Kennington Lane? How many self-identified Ursulas per one-thousand Bears? Had there been a lesbian equivalent to the historical, hysterical, galvanising, generative, prolific, prohibitive, empowering, limiting, liberating, inclusive, exclusive, offensive Gay Zoo? Had there been a Lesbian Zoo? There were lesbian taxonomies sure. But neither Blulip nor P.I. Belahg had heard of a Lesbian Zoo. Blulip, have you? No. No. You?! We could have been fruit flies. Jellyfish. Carnivorous plants. We could have been crystals. There could have been a Lesbian Toxicology. Mineralogy. There probably had been. There probably was.

P.I. Belahg deducted that Blulip's ungulates embodied a proto-queer genealogy *inklusive Pferdefuss.* She considered them critical taxa, with a heightened Ursuline disposition. For P.I. Belahg, their breathless zoo were the Ursuline Ungulates. For P.I. Belahg, Blulip's taxa were the new UUs. The new UUs were Not Quite a new animal. Not Quite a new taxonomy. Not on the level of a Lesbian Mineralogy. But. You know? A start. And who, by the way, is she?! Who's who? There on the floor, next to the bloodstain. Oh, her. Forget *Who's Who*. Who's she!?? Chalk is calcium carbonate or CaCO3. Chalk is porous rock. Chalk is a mineral. Excessively green pigmented.

Fluorescent green chalk outlined an unusually-shaped body on the workshop's linoleum floor. Neon-green, glow-in-the-dark, hi-vis speciality chalk contoured what resembled the reversed flower of a toxic tulip on Blulip's linoleum floor. Toxic Tulep?! Not Tulep. Tulip. The contours of a toxic flower had appeared on linoleum.

The were identical to the contours of the classic icon of a trivialised ghost. Looked like the Pac-Man™ 8-bit green phantom. Rather than the Pink Pac-Man Ghost Machibuse, or the Cyan Pac-Man Ghost Kimagure, this looked like Greenish-Grey Orson. Hello Orson, you greenish-grey, intellectual Ghost. *Was hast du hier verloren?* Allegedly, T. Iwatani, the Japanese video game designer and Pac-Man creator, designed each Pac-Man Ghost with its own distinct personality. Greenish-grey Orson shared with every other Pac-Man Ghost not only the shape of an inverted tulip, but also the outline of a human molar. Two, three or four stumps under a bulbous body. But this was not Orson. This was Orsun Ursol. Orsun Ursol haunted the new UUs. Phantom of Prohibited Futures. Ghost of Taxonomies Yet-to-Come. Millions of taxa would diversify any future taxonomy to the extreme. This was Orsun Ursol, gender-transcender and defender of the *she* pronoun. Neon-green agent of *nouveau*-she. *Nouveau* she-*chique*. Orsun Ursol played a part in the ongoing insurrections of disenfranchised things. Orsun was in cahoots with Peggy and Tulep. Also Healthy-lips, for that matter. Orsun Ursol, you say? CaCO3? Blulip touched her with the tip of her trainer. Blulip tested her with the tip of her trainer. "You're smudging her," Belahg said. Already, Orsun's third foot had gone. P.I. Belahg fetched her smartphone lest Orsun Ursol disappear without record. Using her smartphone, P.I. Belahg was recording Orsun Ursol. "Chalk faery," Blulip said. "It's the scrawl of a chalk faery." It's high-visibility chalk, outlining forensic evidence. It's the chalk outline of a body, like those you see on TV.

A 1996 police audit noted that outlined bodies on TV have taken their toll on modern homicide investigations. Outlining a dead body with chalk or high visibility tape has never been part of official police procedure. Police officers enacting the popular trope has lead to a proliferation of so-called 'chalk faery' contamination of crime scenes with a foreign substance. On rare occasions, officers might have contoured the body or body part at the request of press photographers. The police might have drawn a chalk outline around a body for the press, facilitating family-friendly portrayals of crime scenes. The press had embraced the chalk outline, and so had the literary detective genre. The first time an outline of a body was shown on a television series was in the 1958 Perry Mason episode *The Case Of The Perjured Parrot.* Subsequently the chalk outline had become one of TV's classic tropes, effecting the real world chalk faery proliferation described in the 1996 police audit. Heh, Blulip, Belahg said. Rival investigator Loveday might have contaminated the workshop in our absence. Just saying. P.I. Loveday might have outlined and removed the original body part, Blulip's Maxillary First Molar. Blulip, you know your Maxillary First Molar? Where is it? Exactly. Go figure. Chalk faery Orsun Ursol was replacing Blulip's Maxillary First Molar, significantly affecting the workshop dynamics. *Et zut alors, da haben wir den Salat.* Another suspect/character to reckon with and to consider. Investigative or post-binary lead? What do you think, Blulip?

Deriving from an Ursuline genealogy, spliced with Iwatani's Orson and a helping of faery dust, Orsun Ursol was revitalising a jinxed taxonomy through alien contamination. Orsun Ursol was revitalising the new UUs, their bodily incarnation of a proto-queer past including its problems, through extra-taxonomic freak contamination. Orsun Ursol was revitalising an already contaminated taxonomy through her mineral, digital, media-friendly, computer-gamely, ghostly, intellectual, neon-green, neo-pomp, *nouveau*-she-*chique* version of extra-taxonomic alien contamination. Maybe Orsun was a little flat yet. But she was bound to come alive like everyone else had.

But where was Healthy-lips in all of this? Where was the volatile budgerigar in relation to 'The Perjured Parrot'? Where in relation to Orsun Ursol? Over there! There she was. Suction-cupped to the wall, over there by the kitchen sink. Miles off, really. Healthy-lips was miles away from Orsun Ursol's transgender promise. In terms of the investigation, P.I. Belahg was fairly confident that Tulep, too, was light-years away. Probably Tulep was roaming the Isle of Super-Dykes. That was the kind of old-fashioned bird she was. On that note, Belahg called it a day. Goodnight, Blulip. Goodnight, Belahg. Kiss kiss. Belahg lay down on the floor alongside the kitchenette.

Blulip stayed up. The effect of the oral anaesthetic receded. Orsun Ursol appeared a little less neon-green now. A little more greyish-green. Blulip's thoughts turned to Querbird, her TV series. Amidst queer taxonomies, the new UUs, vanishing Maxillary First Molars and Orsun Ursol, Blulip's thoughts turned to her TV show. On top of Blulip's own improvisations on the script, P.I. Belahg's investigation was interfering with the pre-production process. Also P.I. Loveday's investigation was interfering with the pre-production process, promoting unchecked development, wild-growth and radical off-*piste*ing in terms of the Querbird script. Diversiform investigations facilitated the conditions for the emergence of disenfranchised things in the workshop on Harpur Steet. Riffraff had been running the show from the word go, and they had no regard for the script. They were ever so cocky. They were so prolific. It was questionable whether Blulip's production could ever return to a script.

Especially now they had started filming.

TRANSARMY

Today, P.I. Belagh was wearing her question-mark spangled turtleneck jumper. The blue and green striped turtleneck jumper depicted an army of identical heads in left profile. Red question marks covered or compressed the left-facing heads helmet-like, or clamp-like. A red, left-facing question-mark nestled against each left-facing head from behind. RAF DEMONS/ BLUE & GREEN WOOL PATTERNED TURTLENECK 32287M054002 Long sleeve slim-fit 100% merino wool jumper. Blue/green striped. Head and question-mark pattern throughout in red and orange. Turtleneck collar. Ribbed cuffs and hem. Tonal stitching. Hand wash. Made in Belgium. This was a transgender army. This was an FtM (Female to Male)/T (Trans) army and peace corps. Many were young (not everyone). Many were pretty (not everyone). There were many of them. The head furthest left in the first row from the top was called Nigel. The second, third, fourth, fifth, sixth, seventh, eighth and ninth heads in the first row from the top were called Ralph, Treyvon, Fadel, Hugo, Iqbar, Manfred, Issy, and Koljacz. Issy fancied the back of Koljacz's head. Ralph fancied Treyvon from behind. At first, Manfred did not fancy the new UU Pussycat. Pussycats were not what he usually went for. Neither did Treyvon fancy the Ursuline Bear, who for all he knew might make mincemeat out of him. At first, it looked like the transarmy were cold-shouldering the new UUs. While Belahg was charging her smartphone in the socket by the sink, the transarmy were looking away from the new UUs. The transarmy were looking the exact opposite way. Belahg, too, was looking the other way. Everyone had had enough of the ancient *Pferdefüsse*, the permanent drawbacks. But when Belahg turned her attention to the new UUs and started to record them, the transarmy did a collective U-ey. They could not help but do a U-ey. They did a U-ey because this was a transarmy equipped with question-mark hats. They had a keen interest. Look at Nigel, for example, wearing their question-mark hat. Bristling with herbal testosterone. The transarmy wanted to know their queer history. They wanted to learn about proto-queer. They wanted to know their queer pioneers, and situate their new interventions on transgenerational trans-alliances. So Iqbar did a U-ey. Koljacz did a U-ey. Hugo did a U-ey. And they attacked the new UUs with love. The transarmy tackled the new UUs with interest and love. Conversely, the new UUs tackled the transarmy with love and inquisitive desire. The ensuing scene was not pretty. The ensuing scene was the *Schlachtfeld d'Amour*, the battlefield of love. After hours of fierce engagement, Fadel developed a taste for the new UU Marmoset. Manfred took a special liking to the new UU Afghan. Whereas Ralph continued to fancy Treyvon from behind. On the other hand, Issy fell over himself for Ursol Orsun. Koljacz, too, fell over himself for Ursol Orsun. Whereas Nigel liked heterosexual women, but there weren't any. Far and wide, this was a heterosexual desert. It was not always pretty on the battlefield of love. For a while, it looked as though they might slit each other's throats. Through the lens of Belahg's smartphone, it looked as though the FtM/Ts and the new UUs might slit each other's throats. Eternal turf wars.

In the small hours between 5 and 6am, the battle peaked. Blulip was asleep whilst P.I. Belahg was filming. Inspired by P.I. Loveday, P.I. Belahg was committed to maintaining an up-to-date record of the relevant scene. Having recorded the new UUs at length, P.I. Belahg turned her attention to Healthy-lips. Where was Healthy-lips, her investigative lead? Ah, there. Healthy-lips was standing tall on her singular hoof on the workbench. She looked different today. Had Healthy-lips had an overnight overhaul? A new human bicuspid shone beneath Healthy-lips's beak. Immediately, the transarmy were all over Healthy-lips. They were all over Healthy-lips now. The frontline shifted as Belahg redirected her focus. The frontline now grazed the edge of Healthy-lips's suction-cup. Already Treyvon tackled Healthy-lips with love and inquisitive desire. Iqbar tackled Healthy-lips with love and inquisitive desire. Who are you Healthy-lips, Hugo asked. Who are you today? Baring your tooth like that. What have you become? Healthy-lips had become a battle-axe overnight. Healthy-lips had become a seasoned battle-axe overnight, a hatchet-wielding, uncompromising, unflinching and unforgiving battle-axe. A double-bladed-battle-axe-wielding battle-axe. Combat-tested, and combat-ready. Rigged for the *Schlachtfeld d'Amour*, Healthy-lips was taking no chances. She was ready for horseplay.

Healthy-lips's new and superior tooth stood out against a background of maroon and crimson. Lately, maroon had been mixing with crimson around Healthy-lips's beak, Healthy-lips's mouth. Healthy-lips's lips. Healthy-lips was so anthropomorphic. Healthy-lips, why are you so anthropomorphic? Why are you combat-tested. What battles have you fought? Nigel, Ralph, Treyvon, Fadel, Hugo, Iqbar, Manfred, Issy, and Koljacz were all over Healthy-lips now. Eventually, Blulip got up. Good morning, Belahg *et al*! Good morning, Blulip. P.I. Belahg asked Blulip whether Healthy-lips had been wounded during her battles. P.I. Belahg asked Blulip whether Healthy-lips (during her battles) had lost a lot of blood from the mouth. Blulip shook her head. No. No, Healthy-lips was fine, Blulip replied. If anything, *Blulip* had lost a lot of blood from the mouth during *her* recent battles. "It's maroon-coloured wood glue," Blulip reassured Belahg re. Healthy-lips's suspected blood loss. This, there, around Healthy-lips's mouth, was maroon-coloured wood glue. Maroon-coloured wood glue applied to the reverse of a Maxillary First Bicuspid. The wood glue had smudged a bit. While Belahg had been asleep, Blulip had modified Healthy-lips's mouth area. Blulip had glued her own ex-Maxillary First Bicuspid under Healthy-lips's beak. The accident that had lost Blulip her Maxillary First Bicuspid had also lost her her Maxillary First Molar. The latter had been snatched by the chalk faery. Blulip had managed to recover the former, combing the linoleum floor. Blulip had glued the one tooth that she had lost and that had not been snatched by the chalk faery to Healthy-lips's mouth. Blulip had glued her ex-tooth under Healthy-lips's mouth and turned her into a glorious battle-axe. Strong female lead, Blulip figured. Nigel appeared to agree.

P.I. Belahg was not so sure. She contemplated her investigative lead. Thanks to her newfangled canine, Healthy-lips signified birddog in garish colours. In view of this latest development, P.I. Belahg suspected that Tulep had gone to the Isle of Dogs, or, in fact, to the Canary Islands. In respect of Tulep's compability with the former locale, P.I. Belahg did not think a significant genderqueer presence on the Isle of Dogs likely. She thought a significant genderqueer exodus from the Isle of Dogs more likely. However, performer/director Graham Tornado had platformed transgender presence on the Isle of Dogs's Samuda Housing Estate in her film YHBW (2002). Also, an uncompleted film starring Harvey Keitel had been shot on the same Housing Estate. Harvey Keitel was a popular drag king meme in the 1990s, which would have appealed to Tulep. On the other hand, 16-year-old Lola Rodriguez was the first transgender minor to be nominated for Las Palmas Carnival Queen, Gran Canaria, in February 2015. It was with the one or the other destination in mind, Isle of Dogs or Gran Canaria, that P.I. Belahg suggested they go get some fresh air.

HILARY PARK

The neon-green carpet disintegrated on the forest floor rapidly. The way things were going, it would be integrated in its environment within weeks. The rare flock of sheep *on* the carpet had epigenetically adapted for centuries, alas to another environment. The species had adapted to a faraway rock off the Canarian archipelago. The rock was surrounded by ocean. No grass on it. Over time, the flock had developed an unorthodox physiology hence the ability to metabolise seaweed efficiently. Psychic suction-cups under their hooves had optimised kinaesthesis on their native rock's pebble beach. But this was no pebble beach. This was a forest, *der Schwarzwald,* perhaps, or the Bolivian rain forest. The forest was nowhere near the Canarian archipelago. This was a landlocked state. No ocean for miles. Psychicorporeally disorientated, the flock *stand da wie der Ochs vor dem Berg*. Petrification clouded their acrylic 'flex' eyes. The flock was famished. In this respect, the neon-green carpet was a godsend. It was dyed in a blue-algae derivative. It worked like a survival biscuit for Canarian sheep. Notwithstanding the aftertaste, the flock licked alpaca-mix fibre with gusto. 'Sponsored by *KHelp*™' was printed on the neon-green carpet. *KHelp*™ was a new algae-based soft drink which should not replace a well-balanced diet, but on the occasion it did. It just took the edge off.

Who were these new Ewes!? Who were these new Ewes, in what forest? Any relation to the new UUs at home? Was this a feint? A red herring? Was this the Ewe Forest? But this was not the Ewe Forest. This was not the Black Forest, nor Epping Forest, nor the Bolivian Rain Forest. This was Contamino Park. Impurity Park. Litterland. Carpetland. Unnature Park. Diaspora Park. Desperado Park. Bare-Survival Park. Triumph-over-Tragedy Park. This was a sponsored window display on the Gray's Inn Road, WC1X.

PET CYCLE PLC was an ethical recycling agency for dead animal material. A Private Limited Company, PET CYCLE was an ethical intermediary agency for dead pets, pet parts, and dead animal collectives. Nothing on an industrial scale. With the help of a sponsor (*KHelp*™), Contamino Park was designed to exemplify taxidermy as a practical PetCycle application. Contamino Park exemplified how PetCycling might work for 'you and your pet', to quote from the exhibit label in the shop window. Besides, Contamino Park was designed to promote the sponsor. P.I. Belahg and Blulip were out on a walk. They passed PET CYCLE Head Office, a 110 sq ft shop on the Gray's Inn Road, WC1X, a stone's throw from Harpur Street. The sight of the new window display stopped them in their tracks. Blulip! Hm? Who are these new Ewes?! New UUs/new Ewes, any relation? As soon as P.I. Belahg had caught sight of the new Ewes, she had known she was onto something. Forget the Canaries. Forget the Isle of Dogs. P.I. Belahg had arrived. A bell rang as they entered PET CYCLE Head Office (HO). "Who are they," P.I. Belahg asked re. Contamio Park. "The new Ewes?!" "As good as new," a voice said from within the *faux*-forest. "PetCycled." Behind liana festoons, cardboard palm trees and a real-life office plant, Hilary Park emerged (Park is a common Korean surname). Hilary ran PET CYCLE PLC, had done for years. She was wearing rolled-up jeans and a T-shirt shirt promoting a radical LGBTQI action group, *Helper Cell*. Set of keys on her belt loop. Cherry-red DMs. Hilary was wearing a stylish *Nasir Mazhar* cap with a high-camp pencil holder attached to one side. Under the cap, short hair. Drop of gel in it. Hello, Blulip thought. Butcher than Belahg, Blulip thought. Belahg isn't butch at all. "Hello, Belahg," said Hilary Park. "Belahg, Blulip, hello hello. Nice to see you together. So Gilbert-and-George-like. How is Querbird coming along?" Hilary knew about Blulip's foray into D.I.Y. television. "Not without difficulties," Blulip replied. That's always the way. Isn't that always the way. On the wall behind Hilary, Belahg saw an A4 poster promoting

Blulip's forthcoming Querbird TV series. It had all the right names on it, the necessary credentials. Blulip did not volunteer the fact that the billed author had dropped out of the production. The show had lost its 'name', but Hilary Park was not to know.

Hilary had started PET CYCLE PLC at age 19, from nothing. For 25 years, PetCycle had been facilitating the post-mortem repurposing of pre-compost pets. Hilary's inspiration for PetCycle had been a German PET bottle recycling system, PETCYCLE, that had an almost 100% return rate. In the German context, PET stands for Polyethylene Terephtalite, a polymer resin of the polyester family and constituent of most plastic bottles. Over the last few years, Hilary's PetCycle had skyrocketed in terms of popularity. Like the PET bottle recycling system, Hilary's PetCycle harnessed popular anti-waste sentiments (waste not, want not). Think fossil fuel shortage. Energy crisis. The depleted planet. Think carpet-licking scarcity. PetCycle harnessed the peasantry-come-*haute-cuisine* concept of utilising every part of an animal. There was afterlife in the old dog yet. Think animal fat transformed into biodiesel. PetCycling appealed to pet owners who lacked a back garden. For many, PetCycling compared favourably to burying the dog in a Brockwell Park flowerbed, having her cremated at the Walworth Road vet's, or dumping her in a public bin outside the Tulse Hill housing estate. PetCycling was like *Freecycling,* but ethically supervised. Monthly rotating showcases at PET CYCLE HO illustrated specific PetCycle applications. September 201x: Contamino Park. Tannin, sheepskins, acrylic 'flex' eyes, polyurethane, iron, alpaca-acrylic textile. And courtesy of our sponsor, a free bottle of *KHelp*™ per visitor.

In the absence of a Lesbian Zoo, Contamino Park was second best. This, here, was P.I. Belahg in action. It mattered, and she was ready. P.I. Belahg got her smartphone out. Hilary, look. P.I. Belahg showed yesterday's recording to Hilary. "Who's she?" Hilary asked, meaning Orsun Ursol. "I'm asking you," Belahg said. "You know her?" Hilary tapped her *Nasir Mazhar* cap with high-camp side pencil holder. Mm-hm. Hilary did not know what to suggest in terms of Orsun Ursol, other than to look for her down Brighton pier or Leicester Square Trocadero. Blulip clarified that this was not Orson, Pac-Man's greenish-grey intellectual ghost. This was Orsun Ursol, gender-transcender with faery flair. "I see," Hilary said, "and who's she?" Hilary was referring to Healthy-lips in the background. Oh, Healthy-lips. That's Healthy-lips. Investigative lead, Belahg said. "*Female* lead," Blulip corrected. Blulip preferred to refer to Heathy-lips as the female lead of her TV show. Suddenly Hilary had an idea re Orsun Ursol. It just came to her. Hilary had an idea re whatshername, Orsul Urson. The gender-transcending tooth faery reminded Hilary Park of her lover Rocky Bobák. Orsun reminded Hilary of Bobák for not one, but two reasons. One, Rocky Bobák was a radical gender practitioner. Two, Rocky Bobák was a radical dental practitioner. Hilary was increasingly certain that she saw Bobák in Orsun. Hilary could not now look at Orsun without seeing Bobák. She wrote down Bobák's address. 221 Brixton Hill, SW2. Brixton, Streatham end. "Stay for the launch of Contamino Park?" Hilary asked. Would love to, but could not. Blulip and Belahg would have loved to stay, but they had to go. TV series to produce. Investigation to conduct. *On y va!* They really did have to go. Ok, bye. Bye! They left.

The neon-green carpet disintegrated on the floor of PET CYCLE HO. The *faux*-forest looked suitably wild. The new Ewes had been mounted professionally. Their tongues were stapled to the carpet. Their hooves were screwed to the floor. For the duration of the Contamino Park installation, they were set to stay put. They were unlikely to fall over or lean. Nor were they likely to wander. Unlike Peggy the Pegasus, say, the new Ewes did not ooze *Wanderlust.* Thus it came as a surprise that a new micro-Ewe should be racing across the alpaca-mix carpet. Hilary Park had not expected to find a new micro-Ewe race across the carpet, circling palm tree props. Not on the eve of the launch, she had not. Circa 10 cm in height, the micro-Ewe had a pastel-blue tail-feather. She had tiny hooves. She sprang across the carpet, grazing, apparently. Alpaca-mix fibre was largely inedible, but the neon-green dye was nutrient dense and bioabsorbable. A blue-algae derivative, the dye contained 65 vitamins, minerals and enzymes, eight essential amino acids and ten nonessential amino acids. Spirulina and aphanizomenon flos-aquae are blue algae. Kelps are brown algae. The newfangled micro-Ewe might be seen to inject a little life into the Contamino Park installation. She might be considered the life and soul of the Contamino Party. In theory, something a little less static might lift the Contamino piece. But in reality, the Contamino chimera perplexed and perturbed Hilary Park. Faced with the unlikely micro-Ewe, Hilary Park adjusted her *Nasir Mazhar* cap with the side pencil holder. She looked away and looked back again. The micro-Ewe was still there. Actually, Hilary thought she was seeing things. She re-adjusted her *Nasir Mazhar* cap with high camp side pencil holder for butch reassurance.

TULEP.TV

At Belahg and Blulip's on Harpur Street, the white plastic laptop had moved to the workbench in the living-room/ workshop. Tracey B. Lulip was touch-typing. She registered the domain name Tulep.tv. She installed video streaming software and built a basic website to host a digital TV channel. Blulip ditched the name Querbird. The way her series was going, it would not get a look in at Channel 4. Blulip did not think that her most recent work would wash with Channel 4, not even in Socialist Britain. First, Blulip uploaded the Orsun Ursol footage as a trial. Blulip labelled the footage 'Episode 1', better: the *1st Episode.* The *1st Episode* featured chalk faery/tooth faery Orsun Ursol in improbable detail. Next, Blulip uploaded 'Episode 2', or the *2nd Episode*. No good sitting on your best material. The *2nd Episode* showcased the transarmy in the context of the new UUs and Healthy-lips. Its subtitle: '*Battala d'Amour*'. What now. In contrast to Channel 4, Tulep.tv's audience reach was zero by default. Without promotion, Blulip's content would disappear down the open access black hole. Blulip decided to announce the 'soft launch' of Tulep.tv via her mailing list. Dear Fags and Colleagues. Here's Tulep.tv. Watch the *1st* and *2nd Episodes* now, or catch up later. New episodes every week. Please mark as Not Spam. All Pest, Tracey B. Lulip, Director-General. blulip@tulep.tv.

In fact, Tulep.tv's *1st* and *2nd Episodes* reached a number of viewers, including one ex-mailing list viewer, P.I. Loveday from Holborn Detectives PLC. In keeping with her text-book approach to detective work, P.I. Loveday googled 'Tulep' daily. Hourly. Usually, a link referring to a Turning Lane Extension Project came up, claiming that "TuLEPs are back in active development". That was it. Imagine P.I. Loveday's surprise when Tulep.tv came up. As well as 'Tulep', P.I. Loveday googled 'Gotterbarm' daily. A dental practice for "*integrative Zahnmedizin*" in Hamburg came up: *Zahnarztpraxis* Dr. Gotterbarm, "*[f]ür schöne und gesunde*

Zähne" [accessed 21st September 201x]. Like the Turning Lane Extension Project, P.I. Loveday dismissed this result as insignificant.

ROCKY BOBÀK

Black letters across the shop's brown façade confirmed that this was the NHS *Dental Repair Shop Rocky Bobák*. The brown façade suggested a funeral parlour or a pawnshop, say, but black letters confirmed that this was the NHS *Dental Repair Shop ___k_ ___ák*, or ______ *___air _hop ___k_ ___ák*, to be precise. Several letters were missing. Formerly self-adhesive brown film furled up in both bottom corners of the shop window. Ok, Blulip said. Let's go in. You first, Belahg said. Together? Ok.

P.I. Belahg was wearing her question-marks jumper with her Y-3 *Hero* joggers. Blulip was wearing her white/orange shark-print T-shirt with her camouflage joggers from *Tesco*. From *Christopher Ala*'s AW1x collection, Blulip's T-shirt was featuring tiny sharks swimming in concentric circles. Wonderfully soft cotton, and a bold shark print throughout. Inside, Blulip, Belahg *et al* encountered an NHS self-service check-in kiosk. This might take a while. Blulip did not have her appointment letter with her. Neither did Ralph, Treyvon, Fadel, Hugo, Iqbar, Manfred, Nigel, Issy and Koljacz from the FtM/T collective have their appointment letters at hand. The sharks were without appointment letter between them. Not to mention Belahg. Belahg suggested that Blulip go first. Together? Blulip asked. No. You're on your own. Ok. The self-service check-in kiosk asked Blulip for her name. Blulip typed 'Tracey Biryukov Lulip', her full name. The kiosk asked whether Blulip was male or female and what were her ambitions. Blulip responded by entering a 'Spinning Heart' emoticon. The kiosk, in return, proliferated 'Triple Heart' emoticons on its screen before crashing.

P.I. Belahg, Blulip, Ralph, Treyvon, Fadel, Hugo, Iqbar, Manfred, Nigel, Issy, Koljacz and hundreds of sharks entered the *DRS* waiting room. Dental glue fumes stalled the breath reflex. Circa thirty *DRS* patients lined the walls, waiting for their turn and the return of their previously deposited dentures. Avoiding interaction and eye contact (try saying ts, or pf, without dentures), the patients concentrated on an unsual Art Deco tessellation design on the waiting room carpet.

Belahg and Blulip sat down on adjacent chairs. Blulip, look! Hm? There! Where? Belahg gestured towards the shop window that connected the waiting room via brown self-adhesive film to Brixton Hill. At a desk in the shop window, Rocky Bobák was fixing dental prosthetics. Rocky Bobák was wearing joggers, T-shirt, and *adidas* trainers. She wore large, black-rimmed glasses. Blulip, see? Oh yeeaah. With a specialist spatula, Rocky Bobák was applying *Fixodent*™ denture glue to the cracked Perspex palate of a partial denture. Dental paraphernalia littered the desk's work surface. Sixteen pots of *Fixodent*™ in as many colours did not cover the *DRS*'s clientele's diverse gum complexion spectrum. Now Bobák scrutinised the partial denture in the light of a desk lamp. Shiny metal strands as well as a single incisor extended from the object's Perspex component. It resembled a fleshy mass, or a dermoid cyst complete with ingrown silver hair and tooth. Must feel like barbed wire in the mouth, Blulip imagined, remembering the gaps in her own set of teeth. Seemingly satisfied with her handiwork, Bobák left the glued denture to dry. She looked up the next patient on her laptop. DOB 12/12/1974. "That's us," Belahg said to Blulip.

Bobák searched for Blulip's files on her laptop. "Can I help?" Bobák looked at Belahg and Blulip. "Who are you, Gilbert and George? And who are they." "Transarmy and peace corps," Belahg said apropos of Bobák's second question. Some of the generally disenfranchised powers that ran this show. "Ah ok," Bobák said. "Hilary sent us," Belahg said. "Hilaire!" Bobák cried. "Did you go to the launch of Contamino Park at PET CYCLE HO last night?" "No, you?" "No." "Hilary thought you might be able to help." Streaming Tulep.tv on her smartphone, P.I. Belahg played Bobák the 2nd *Episode* first. "What's this," Bobák asked. "Healthy-lips, you say? Strong peg. Can I buy her? Great on my desk. Would make for a nice *DRS* mascot, patron saint, *Leitfigur*. How much? And what's this, looks nasty." "Oh this," Belahg said. "The battlefied *d'Amour.*" "What?! The battlefied *d'Amour*?!" Ralph, Treyvon, Fadel, Hugo, Iqbar, Manfred, Nigel, Issy and Koljacz kept quiet. Then P.I. Belagh showed Bobák the footage of Orsun Ursol. "Hilary thought you might recognise her?" No, Bobák did not recognise Orsun Ursol. However, Orsun Ursol reminded Rocky Bobák of Rocket Bazcjk. Rocket Bazcjk was Rocky Bobák's *nouveau*-drag alter ego. The way that Orsun had painted her fingernails, for example, reminded Bobák of the way that Rocket Bazcjk painted her fingernails. Or were these Orsun's toenails? These were blood splatters on my linoleum floor, Blulip objected. These were blood splatters surrounding Orsun Ursol, not nail varnish. "I had an accident," Blulip explained, indicating her mouth. "Prospective *DRS* mascot swooped from the ceiling, knocking my teeth out." "I see," Bobák said. "Bobák, can you help?" Blulip asked.

Dentures are made from Polymethylmethacrylate (PMMA). PMMA is acrylic Perspex, or Plexiglas. The skeletal formula for acrylic Perspex is:

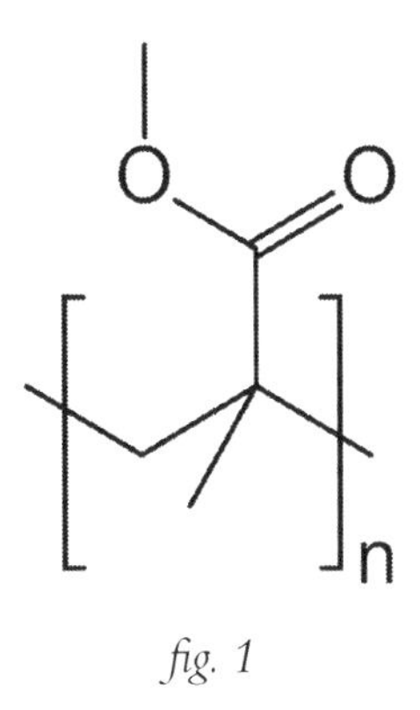

fig. 1

"Aha," P.I. Belahg observed, "it says loon." From top left (l), down and across (oo), to bottom right (n). P.I. Belahg thought it said loon. Whereas the transarmy saw the face of an aggressive bird. The transarmy saw the face of battle-axe Healthy-lips. See the tooth (n) under her beak? Bottom right? The tooth (n) under Healthy-lips's beak made the FtM/Ts tetchy. But the aggressive bird was not Healthy-lips. She was the Acrylic Pecker. The Acrylicker. The Acrylicker?! NO. Blulip was not having any of it. The world did not need another bird right now. The world did not need the Acrylicker, and it certainly did not need the Acrylic Pecker. Blulip rejected the Acrylicker alongside PMMA, Perspex, or Plexiglas. Seeing the dermoid-cyst-like denture drying on Bobák's desk, Blulip had been developing an aversion to Perspex. A Plexiglas allergy. In terms of her dental replacement, Perspex was not an option for Blulip. Blulip was clear on that. Scanning the desk for alternatives, Blulip came across this jollier figure. "Who's this," Blulip asked.

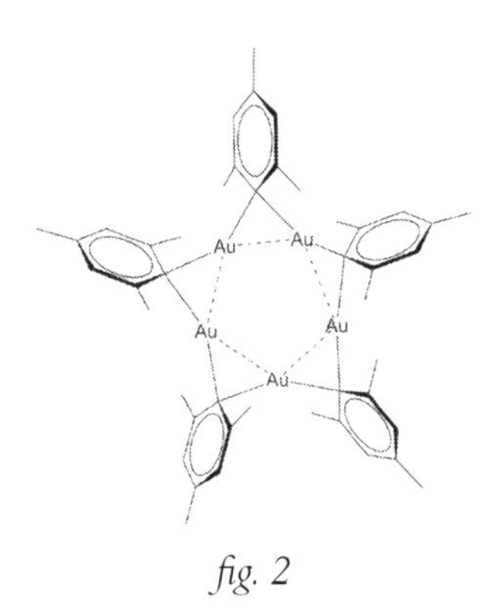

fig. 2

Who was this jollier figure? A butch ballerina performing an arabesque? A femme ballerino? An arabesque is a pose in ballet in which the dancer stands on one leg with the other leg extended behind the body. An arabesque can be executed with the supporting leg *en pointe*, *demi pointe* or with foot flat on the floor. Did the femme ballerino execute her arabesque with the supporting leg *en pointe*, or did she just happen to have pointy feet? And wasn't this also the formula for the chemical element gold? Rocky Bobák, you couldn't manufacture a GOLD CROWN for Blulip?! Blulip perferred the butch ballerina over the Acrylicker any day. But Bobák objected in terms of *fig. 2.* This was not a femme ballerino. Neither was it the skeletal formula for the chemical element gold, in spite of its similar appearance. This was *Colt*, not gold. The fivefold symmetrical sketch on Bobák's desk represented Colt, not gold. "This," Bobák insisted in respect to the butch ballerina, "is Colt." Colt lived in the back, apparently. "If you wait, I'll show you." "Oh. Ok." "Ok." "Let's wait."

Inevitably, Colt replaced gold as the narrative focus. The narrative diverted away from a prospective gold crown for Blulip because of Colt (who?). Both, the ballet dancer executing an arabesque and the chemical element gold had been criminally outperformed by this Colt. It was all about Colt now. Once the last patient had been dealt with, Rocky Bobák lead Belahg, Blulip, the FtM/T legion, and hundreds of previously inconsequential sharks to the tiny D.I.Y. laboratory where Colt lived.

COLT

The fivefold symmetrical organism was held in the apparatus under-part uppermost. Hundreds of miniscule tube feet pedalled on empty. The o-shaped mini-mouth gasped for oxygen, or attacked space in self-defence. The sea urchin's teeth are self-sharpening and can chew through stone. Five minuscule milk fangs are typically arranged inside a circular lip, with a fleshy tongue-like structure within. The animal model in the laboratory spanner had substandard oral health. She retained merely two of five crystalline cuspids. Too much chewing on stone, or not enough. Or had the fluctuating pH levels of South London tap water affected her dental enamel? "Almost done," Rocky Bobák said, carefully cleaning the 2mm orifice with a filament implement, a human hair. "Say aah."

"Cute," Blulip said, referring to Bobák.

Global experimental activity around human tooth regeneration had been increasing over the last decade, Bobák explained. The shared objective was the production of modified human gum cells capable of third generation odontogenesis. Humans grow 52 teeth in thrusts of 20 (milk) and 32 (permanent). Then it stops. Finito. The stemcell-laden layer of tissue in the gum that provides the impetus for tooth growth goes into latency. The Franco/Brazilian team that led the contemporary global research effort concentrated on alligators and their capacity to grow up to 4thousand new teeth, birth-to-death. Sharks grow up to 24thousand. A hundred sharks on Blulip's *Christopher Ala* T-shirt grew 2.4 million between them. Compared to other prolific tooth-producers, the alligator's dental anatomy most closely resembles the human's. The alligator's dental anatomy is basically humanesque. Alligators, however, make for impractical lab rats. Particularly in central Brixton. Imagine, Bobák said.

Odontogenesis, or tooth development, is a complex and species-specific process from initiation to eruption that depends on gene expression, protein signalling, cell functions,and unknown factors. Growth and morphogenesis of human teeth, for example, are regulated by the Sonic Hedgehog protein. Discovered in 1980 in Heidelberg, the Sonic Hedgehog protein is encoded in the Sonic Hedgehog gene whose loss of function causes fruit-fly embryos to grow hedgehog-like spikey projections. Hence the name. Sonic Hedgehog, abbreviated to SHh. Shh! Say nothing but. Sonic Hedgehog's centrality to human odontogenesis might have inspired Rocky Bobák's unorthodox choice of test organism. German for 'sea urchin' is '*Seeigel*' which literally translates as 'sea hedgehog'. Shh. Say nothing but. Bobák's choice of test organism might have been based on a pun.

Since 1991, Rocky Bobák had been experimenting with *eccinoidea* specimens in the D.I.Y. lab at the back of the *Dental Repair Shop.* Nice sideline. Yes. Sea urchins have a fivefold symmetrical structure, look. Structurally gold-like. Look, Blulip. See now? Colt, not gold. Golden biotechnological possiblities. *Eccinoidea* teeth never cease growing. Might sea urchin odontogenesis, fully understood, provide the biochemical tools to transform mainstream prosthodontics? Bobák just put this to Belahg. But the golden days of Bobák's box room lab were over, apparently. After 20 years of research activity and numerous controversial contributions to her field, Bobák had pared down her laboratory facilities in 2011. An orthodontically atypical, one-in-a-million specimen remained, at present resisting her routine dental check-up. Her name was Colt, evocative of a young stallion. "Bobák, would you call Colt a formidable micro-stallion?" P.I. Belahg mooted. Personally, Rocky Bobák would not call Colt a formidable micro-stallion, but she supposed that one might. "All done," Bobák said, releasing Colt from the spanner. Bobák dropped her model organism into a conical test flask with a large diameter cylindrical neck. Technically, a fishbowl.

Ok, Bobák said. Let's start. Watch this. Under the watchful eyes of her guests, Rocky Bobák fed Colt kelp.

Rocky Bobák plopped Colt a densely compressed, algae-blue tablet of kelp. Plop. Fizzed in the fishbowl. Blulip stood near the front. Belahg and the FtM/T peace corps kept in the background. Plop, fizz. Then nothing. The shiver of sharks on Blulip's *Christopher Ala* T-shirt appeared to hold Colt in check. The shiver of sharks appeared to affect Colt's appetite. The shiver of sharks on Blulip's *Christopher Ala* T-shirt frightened the living daylights out of Colt, effectively ruining her appetite. Meanwhile, a shark on Blulip's back hooked onto Hugo. Hugo's hook-like cap drove the shark crazy. Hugo and his hook piqued the shark's appetite. Another shark on Blulip's back hooked onto Iqbar. Iqbar and their hook drove the shark crazy and piqued its appetite. Under threat of a shark attack, Iqbar and Nigel came alive. They were the liveliest of the FtM/T lot. Now Iqbar and Nigel appeared to egg Colt on. Come on, Colt. Have a go. Go on! Belahg joined Iqbar and Nigel. She stepped to the front, rooting for Colt. But oh. Oh no. If only Belahg had stayed in the background. Belahg should have stayed in the background, she should have lain low.

Because now Colt hooked onto Nigel. Nigel's hook-like cap drove Colt crazy. Nigel's hook piqued Colt's appetite. Nigel's hook piqued the appetite of a wilder animal. Colt's dental decrepitude turned tiger-like attitude. As a consquence, Colt bit off more than she could chew. Colt bit off a lot more than she could chew. Overextending herself, she buckled like an infatuated micro-stallion.

THE GOLDSEXUAL STATUETTE

A GoldSeXUal StatuEtte manoeuvred herself across the workshop wearing a gold crown on one head, and a *Nasir Mazhar* cap with a side pencil holder on the other. Left, the GoldSeXUal StatuEtte's *Nasir-Mazhar*-cap-wearing head instructed the GoldSeXUal StatuEtte's crown-wearing head. Ok, stop. Who was the GoldSeXUal StatuEtte and what was she actioning? The GoldSeXUal StatuEtte incorporated Hilary, Blulip, and the new UU's DNA and AgeNDa, merging several post-binary sexes and projects. Right now, GoldSeXUal's *Nasir-Mazhar*-cap-wearing head kissed the naked light bulb. GoldSeXUal's crown-wearing head was actively turning away from Hilary's groin. Meanwhile, P.I. Belahg recorded GoldSeXUal's excesses on her smartphone. Heh, GoldSeXUal StatuEtte, Belahg called. Are you a frame-of-reference-stretcher in the sex and gender department? Are you the Gold Standard of radical sexes? Haha, GoldSeXUal laughed. GoldSeXUal did not think that she was the Gold Standard of radical sexes. Belahg filmed her anyway. Heh, GoldSeXual, Belahg reiterated.The GoldSeXUal StatuEtte preferred the address 'Sxuse'.The GoldSeXUal StatuEtte said that she preferred the address 'Sxuse' at all costs. Sxuse, pronounced 'Zeus'. Or simply Susi. Ok, Belahg said. GoldSeXUal cried that she had to screw something else now.The *Nasir-Mazhar*-cap-wearing head informed the crown-wearing head that GoldSeXUal had some extra screwing to do at the other end of the workshop. Dangerously, the GoldSeXUal StatuEtte set herself into motion. GoldSeXUal got herself into gear. Belagh leapt onto the workbench and recorded the feat. For movement's sake, GoldSeXUal's crown-wearing head pushed right into Hilary's groin. Hilary's groin was GoldSeXUal's crown-wearing head's natural disposition.

GoldSeXual's crown-wearing head looked like Blulip's, and GoldSeXual's *Nasir-Mazhar*-cap-wearing head looked like Hilary Park's. GoldSeXUal's body or principal mass looked like Hilary Park balancing on the back of the fibreglass Cygnet, and Blulip clasping Hilary's legs for support.

'Scuse! Belahg exclaimed. The GoldSeXUal StatuEtte, or Sxuse, ploughed through the new UUs. GoldSeXUal barged into non-participant fibreglass animals.

It was Princess Blulip's fault. Belahg believed that Sxuse's barging into bystanders was Princess Blulip's fault. The GoldSeXUal StatuEtte was navigationally unreliable what with her crown-wearing head (Blulip's) buried in Hilary's groin. Heh, Princess Blulip! Belahg called. The GoldSeXUal StatuEtte froze. "Don't," Blulip said. "Don't call me 'Princess'." Blulip let go of Hilary's legs and confronted Belahg. "Call me the Great Camp King Pin, if you must," Blulip said. Blulip had the great British novelist Brigid Brophy to thank for this title (*In Transit,* 1969). If Blulip was not part of the GoldSeXUal StatuEtte, she was the Great Camp King Pin. NOT Princess Blulip. See that crown?! It's a camp king thing. It's not a tiara. Ok, Belahg said. A camp king thing. Belahg was sorry she had referred to the Great Camp King Pin as 'Princess Blulip'. Satisfied, the G.C.K.P. resumed her position as the GoldSeXUal StatuEtte's crown-wearing head and navigational motor. Normality returned quickly. The GoldSeXUal StatuEtte as a whole did not invest in localised tantrums.

To return to the question, who was the GoldSeXUal StatuEtte and what was she actioning: The GoldSeXUal StatuEtte combined long-term queer activisms (new UU), queened-up agenderism (Blulip), and no-fucks-giving butchness (Hilary) into a post-binary, extra-individual, socio-biological sex and a transformative gender. The GoldSeXUal StatuEtte was pushing the sexual envelope, as well as the boundaries of performance art, criminal investigation, indie TV production, and D.I.Y.. Over the course of her goldSeXUal escapades, the GoldSeXUal StatuEtte effected adequate lighting in Blulip's studio/ workshop. Already the GoldSeXUal StatuEtte had fixed many finicky light fittings. She was working her goldSeXUal magic at the far end of the workshop right now. The GoldSeXUal StatuEtte was fixing light fittings for Britain.

Blulip had hoped that the initiative would improve the quality of Tulep.tv's materials. It did, and not just in terms of image resolution. Just look at the latest video going up. The *3rd Episode* featured the GoldSeXUal StatuEtte in conversation with an offscreen interrogator (P.I. Belahg). Within half an hour of it going live, real-life Peggy Shaw had left a comment in Tulep.tv's designated section. With Lois Weaver and Deb Margolin, Peggy Shaw (1944-) was a founding member of lesbian/queer performance troupe *Split Britches* (1980-). Peggy Shaw posted this picture in the comments section: *fig. 3*. Next, real-life Lois Weaver Replied To This Post: "In terms of post-binary hybrids, *Split Britches* performed *this* in 1995: 'A Transgender Arabesque'. Their comments were not about copyright.

fig. 3

Within an hour of the *3rd Episode* going live, the doorbell rang in the workshop on Harpur Street. The GoldSeXUal StatuEtte opened the door. Outside, the Transgender Arabesque. The GoldSeXUal StatuEtte's *Nasir-Mazhar-*

cap-wearing head and her crown-wearing head faced the Transgender Arabesque's permanent wave sporting head. *Vice versa*, the Transgender Arabesque's permanent wave sporting head faced the GoldSeXUal StatuEtte's *Nasir-Mazhar*-cap-wearing head and her crown-wearing head. The Transgender Arabesque wore a gown fit for a princess. A leg dressed in suit trousers and shoes extended from the Transgender Arabesque's gown.

An arabesque is one of the basic poses in classical ballet. The term 'arabesque' is an orientalism unfortunately, deriving from the 17th Century French/Italian perception of a type of pattern elemental to Pre-Islamic and Islamic art. From the French and Italian perspectives, patterns of scrolling and interlacing foliage, tendrils or thin stems captured the sensibility of the ballet pose.

"Nice brogue," the GoldSeXUal StatuEtte said. Also, "nice gown." "Ta," the Transgender Arabesque (aka TA) replied. "Why have you got a GOLD CROWN on?" The Transgender Arabesque questioned GoldSeXUal's crown rather than GoldSeXUal's *Nasir Mazhar* cap with the high camp side pencil holder. "To keep the Acrylicker at bay," GoldSeXUal's crown wearing head replied. "I see," the Transgender Arabesque said. To return to the hydra-headed question, who was the GoldSeXUal StatuEtte and what was she actioning, she was Blulip fixating on an improbable gold crown in *lieu* of her Maxillary First Bicuspid, Maxillary First Molar, or Perspex dentures. She was P.I. Belahg pursuing a neglected gold crown lead. She was P.I. Belahg and Blulip running with a throw-away gold crown mention, see chapter 'ROCKY BOBÀK'. She was Hilary Park fixing light fittings for Britain, too.

"GoldSeXUal StatuEtte," the Transgender Arabesque said. "GoldSeXUal StatuEtte, do exploit your photogenicity for Tulep.tv." The Transgender Arabesque showed her experiencedness in the entertainment industry here. "If you don't want Tulep.tv to go under, do exploit your photogenicity and personal charisma." The Transgender Arabesque tried to prevent Tulep.tv's sinking without a trace. What other capital was there? Monetary? Cracking script? Performance background? No. None of the aforementioned. "Have you explored sex-radical role play, cabaret, or lip-synching satire?" "Not yet. Cheap innuendo. Camp comedy. *C'est ça.*" Camp comedy?! The Transgender Arabesque shook her Lois-head. "Not good. Not good at all. Let me help. Let me demonstrate." The Transgender Arabesque engaged the GoldSeXUal StatuEtte in sex-radical role playing. Oho! P.I. Belahg could not believe what was happening live on her smartphone screen. She could not believe what she was filming. The Transgender Arabesque and the GoldSeXUal StatuEtte engaging in sex-radical role play was better than cheap innuendo. Better than camp comedy. Better than Querbird and Channel 4. This was TV GOLD. Even P.I. Belahg knew TV gold when she saw it.

'GoldSeXUal StatuEtte meets Transgender Arabesque' was a six minute clip, uploaded in the comment section of the *3rd Episode.* Within hours, the clip accrued a record number of viewings. Already, its viewing figures exceeded the *1st* and *2nd Episode*s' combined viewing numbers. Lively debate in the comments section too (not about copyright). Only then did Director-General Tracey B. Lulip promote the clip to *4th Episode.* On second thoughts, the *4th Episode* was not captioned 'GoldSeXUal StatuEtte meets Transgender Arabesque'. Rather, it was captioned 'Transgender Arabesque *cruises* GoldSeXUal StatuEtte'. But that wasn't it either. Blulip went further still. The *4th Episode* was captioned 'Peggy Shaw and Lois Weaver (*Split Britches*) cruise Hilary Park (PET CYCLE)'. Blulip was a quick learner. Something about discoverability. About Googleability, and online traction.

PRINCESS DIANA

Googling variations on 'princess', 'misidentify princess', and 'mistake princess identity', P.I. Belahg came across a report entitled 'Tourist Joins Search Party for Herself in Hyde Park'. The report had circulated on the typical social networking sites in April 2016 and again in July 201x:

A coach draws up at the Princess Diana Memorial Fountain in Hyde Park, London. International tourists get off the bus and freshen up in the rest rooms. A tourist decides to update her outfit. She changes from her *Rubchinskiy* Black Polar Bears T-shirt into a *C&A* Concentric Circles T-shirt. When the tourist gets back on the bus, her fellow travellers fail to recognise her *sans* Black Polar Bears T-shirt. Word spreads that someone is missing. The tourist fails to recognise the missing-person's description as a description of herself. A major search operation around Hyde Park is mobilised, including dogs and a helicopter. Police divers search the Serpentine and the Memorial Fountain itself. The tourist in question is amongst those most invested in the search. She emerges as an operational driving force. 14 hours into the operation, one of the tour operators counts the passengers on a hunch. The tour operator confirms the group's completeness. The search is called off with immediate effect.

P.I. Belahg identified with the subject of the report immediately. P.I. Belahg *was* the tourist in the *Rubchinskiy* Black Polar Bears T-shirt and the *C&A* Concentric Circles T-shirt. Like the deplorable tourist, P.I. Belahg had not realised that she had been the subject of her own investigation. Like the international tourist, P.I. Belahg had been unaware that she had been the subject of her own search and investigation. Now, P.I. Belahg realised who Belá Gotterbarm was. Who *she* was. P.I. Belahg *was* Belá Gotterbarm. And Belá Gotterbarm was P.I. Belahg. With a new sense of entitlement, Belahg got up and walked into the bedroom. She crossed P.I. Loveday's pink cordon and picked up a discarded sweater. She took off her RAF DEMONS question-marks jumper, and replaced it with the new sweater. It featured a Pegasus print, and it fitted to a t.

P.I. Belahg sat down on the hound's-tooth Formica table that stood by the window. The Pegasus on Belahg's sweater reared and raised her wings. Pink flashes and green graffiti manifested Pegasus energy. Pegasus energy, perhaps, powered P.I. Belahg's subsequent meditations. Her thought process connected Tulep to Colt, Colt to Tulep.

1) In one chapter, a formidable micro-horse had sprung across the Formica tabletop. Tulep had postured atop the Formica tabletop like a feminine mini-stallion.

2) A colt is a young stallion, a male foal. Colt had buckled like an infatuated female stallion.

3) Healthy-lips signified TOOTH, in capital letters. Tulep's proxy Healthy-lips signified TOOTH, which might or might not indicate the Isle of Dogs, or the Canaries.

4) Dental health was a determining factor in Colt's life, and integral to her persona.

That's how P.I. Belahg produced the hypothesis that Tulep and Colt were identical. Colt *was* Tulep. And Tulep was Colt.

On second thought, did Colt have hooves? Pinions? P.I. Belahg could not be sure. Verifying this latest hypothesis would go beyond testing the fit of a sweatshirt. Verifying Colt's identity would require a face-to-face confrontation and a recce to Rocky Bobàk's *DRS* laboratory. A top secret moonlight operation was on the agenda. Blulip! Belahg called. What are you doing later?

MÖRDERVOGEL

P.I. Belahg was wearing her *Comme Des Garçons* shirt with Mexican-inspired pompom detailing fringing the button tab and the chest pocket. Bottle-green/turquoise chequered poplin. 100% polyester pompoms. Belahg was wearing her shirt with her *Y-3 Hero* joggers. Blulip was wearing her *Christopher Ala* white/orange shark-print T-shirt and her camouflage patterned joggers from *Tesco*. She wore the cuffs of her joggers tucked into a pair of gold-threaded socks. A person on the 59 bus complimented them on their Gilbert-&-George-like aesthetics and sensibility. People were so educated in Socialist Britain. At 11 pm, P.I. Belahg and Blulip got off at Brixton Hill, Streatham end. They broke into Rocky Bobák's laboratory. It was easy. The backdoor was inadequately secured. When it came to it, Blulip preferred to wait outside. You don't mind, Belahg, do you? Blulip preferred to wait by the energy-saver emergency lamp near the entrance, rather than enter the barely-lit lab. You go in, Blulip said. Go on. In you go. Ok, P.I. Belahg ventured forth.

On a shelf ahead, a liquid lampion expended a golden lustre. Aha! A conical laboratory flask (Colt's fishbowl) fluke-reflected Blulip's gold-threaded socks in the distance. Exploiting the fluke for the purpose of her investigation, P.I. Belahg navigated her partner to shed light on her mission, to spotlight the fishbowl in question. "Blulip, step to the left! Left! No, left!?" Despite her efforts, Belahg's research object continued to fluctuate between one too many realities. Belahg couldn't see. "Blulip! Left is where your thumb is on your right!" Blulip said to use the smartphone as a torch. Why not use the torch app on your phone? Ah. O-keh, Belahg said. Make a video, too. Quick! Belahg got her phone out. "Blulip?" "Hm?" "How can you tell whether a sea urchin is dead?" Belahg zoomed in on the fishbowl's content. "Flip her over. If you look right in the middle, you will see five little shapes that look like teeth. If they move, she's alive." [*Yahoo! Answers*, accessed 2nd Sept, 201x.] P.I. Belahg slipped her free hand through the cylindrical neck and into the test flask. She flipped Colt over and investigated. Tulep? Is that you?

A fan came on in the corner. What sounded like a fan catching its casing came on in the corner. Blulip wanted to go. Belahg, let's go. "Wait," Belahg said, recording the fishbowl's content. "I lost a pompom in there." A Mexican-style pompom was floating inside the flask, a turquoise polyester boat drifting like flotsam and jetsam. Are you joking. Belahg, are you joking? Blulip was panicking. The fan stopped. A terrible flapping ensued in the corner, like a large bird's wings pounding their concrete confinement. *K-RACH K-RAACH*. What's that?! *K-RAAACH*! Blulip and Belahg abandoned their midnight recce and legged it.

Terminating her flight, Tulep settled next to the fishbowl. The pompom inside was a gift after Tulep's own heart. Her owner Belá Gotterbarm/P.I. Belahg had left a pompom for her. In the absence of basic animal care and ownerly love, a pompom from Belá Gotterbarm/P.I. Belahg came a close second. Tulep was orbiting her *Faszinationsobjekt* like a formidable mini-filly. She pranced against the fishbowl like a young colt. With the resolve of a feminine stallion, she finally went for it. Tulep succeeded in overturning the fishbowl. The result wasn't pretty, but the pompom was. It swam in a pool on the laboratory floor. Tulep picked up the pompom using her beak where it would remain until further notice.

Right, where did they go. Tulep exited through the window, and went after Gotterbarm/P.I. Belahg. Since returning from her sojourn on the Isle of Dykes, dogging her feckless owner had become a mode of existence for Tulep.

ICY PET

The pink, brown and coffee-cream peony pattern was based on an Art Deco tessellation design. Variously shaped straight-edged pink petals clustered around coffee-cream reproductive centres into four variations of a peony flower. Variously shaped straight-edged coffee-cream petals clustered around pink reproductive centres into four spectrally inverted variations of a peony flower. The pink/coffee-cream and coffee-cream/pink peonies were arranged and replicated across the polyester carpet in such a way that the brown interspaces between individual peonies added up to a straight-edged multi-lizard-shaped labyrinth, sinkhole or sewer. In addition to that, the coffee-cream elements added up to a quasi-SOS in 2D, a Morse code distress signal smeared across polyester.

The carpet covering the waiting room floor was integral to the ethos and the aesthetics of *Dental Repair Shop Rocky Bobák*. It shaped its collective imaginary. It also needed replacing. It had needed replacing since circa 1975. The window however in which to replace it had closed. In 1976 the carpet had been included in the English Heritage Statutory List of Structures of Special Interest on grounds not of the Art Deco *pièce unique,* but the material depicting it. Pivotally positioned within the history of industrial innovations, Bobák's floor-covering was not your average Axminster but a rare polyester prototype produced in 1939. Polyester had not been officially invented until 1941, when PolyEthylene Terephthalate (PET) had been patented in Britain. PET had formed the basis of *Terylene®,* the first synthetic fibre to be commercially manufactured by Imperial Chemical Industries (ICI). PET, ICI. Icy pet. But not yet. The prototypical exemplar of PET had been put forward by a West-Indian chemical laboratory in 1939. A Western rival laboratory however had persuaded the scientific community that the West-Indian innovation was carcinogenic. Derivative of a previous failure, failure for all sorts of reasons. The rival had ended up patenting their identical version of PET, but not until 1941, two years later. Delaying Icy Pet. They delay/I delay Icy Pet. Has it been said that the pink/brown and coffee-cream Art Deco tessellation pattern in proto-polyester produced yet another figure, in *Vogelperspektive* (bird's eye view)? A larger figure. Dadaist, even. The *König der Vögel,* a large-bodied turkeyheader, reared her head over so many pink-brown-and-coffee-cream peonies that crowded like individual organs around and within her. Carrying the air and skin-tone of a turkey in the freezer compartment, the original Icy Pet held her head up and raised her arms in defiance. This was *der König der Vögel*, the Icy Pet, or her of the priceless pink-brown-and-coffee-cream polyester polyphony. Whatever next.

Peopling the infamous rug was Bobák in gladrags. This was Bobák in drag. Bobák was wearing her Rocket Bazcjk *alter ego.* She was getting in touch with her feminine side. Her ensemble comprised a traditional Black Forest dress under a punky T-shirt, a pair of knee-length, multi-coloured socks depicting butterflies, flowers and genitalia-shaped insects and worms, black hairclips in her blond boy's haircut, and burgundy lipstick on her mouth and forehead. On the alternative scene, she had won prizes. A John-Waters-inspired double drag introvert, Rocket Bazcjk was mending gum-coloured palates at her desk in the shop window. Highly functioning, she routinely performed technical labour while evaluating the day's *nouveau*rthodontic procedures, or formulating those of tomorrow. Tonight however was special. Rocket Bazcjk was wearing her *Helper Cell* T-shirt on top of her traditional dress. The T-shirt had been in a moth bag for over a decade. It owed its current airing to Rocket-knew-not-what, the multi-lizard-shaped shit channel underfoot, the blatant coffee-cream S.O.S., the original Icy Pet's pushing a defiant agenda. The fact that she had seen someone on Coldharbour Lane yesterday wearing hers. As it were, the John-Waters-and-polyester-affinitive double-dragger wearing an original *Helper Cell* T-shirt constituted just one manifestation of a larger-scale, slow-starter, multi-tiered insurrection of helpers to come.

Around midnight, Belahg and Blulip knocked against the shop window. A 'helper' sat at her work desk, repairing dental prostheses. Hello Bazcjk, Belahg, Blulip, hello hello. How nice to, nice T-shirt. Come on in. "You might want to sit down, Rocket," Blulip said as they entered the waiting room. Belahg and Blulip were here officially to inform Rocket Bazcjk of the discovery they had made in Rocky Bobàk's laboratory. "My laboratory? Do break into the back entrance, why don't you!" "Sorry," Belahg said. Then Blulip reported that Bobák's model specimen, experimental indispensable, and long-term companion animal Colt was dead. Belahg and Blulip had found her extinct in her fishbowl. The pink, brown and coffee-cream peony variations on Rocket's polyester appeared positively lively, Blulip explained, compared to the way that the animal had presented when Belahg had close-examined her less than an hour ago. In terms of tooth movement, Colt's mini-mouth had stood agape post-last-gasp. A hundred sharks had been present to no effect. A hundred *Christopher Ala* sharks on white cotton had had zero animating effect on Colt. Colt was dead. Our condolences, Blulip concluded. We truly are sorry. Oh dear. Oh no. Was there anything else?! Peony peony, lizardine shite. Pink-brown polyester reality, stay *unterschwellig*, stay out of it. But merciless Icy Pet showed her coffee-creamed features and body in polyester, commencing her intervention. Icy Pet's hands appeared larger than average, her digits swollen. Yes, Blulip said. Now that you mention it, there *was* something else. Belahg and Blulip were in a position to confirm that something or someone else had been in the laboratory who might be connected to Colt's demise. Something or someone had interfered with their forensic inventory, had in fact precipitated their inventory's abortion. A faceless threat had beaten her flight feathers in a corner under the ceiling. "Flight feathers? What else." Peony, peony, lizardine interference. Pink, brown and coffee-cream poly-reality… Yes, flight feathers. Like Max Ernst's Loplop, or, come to think of it, the very coffee-cream Icy Pet there, the faceless flapper had had multiple tentacles terminating in hands with balloony digits. Newfangled strangle instruments, Blulip intimated. Killing machines. Also flight-enabling, dual functional. "What?!" Murder flutterer, *Mördervogel*. She probably done it. Bazcjk frowned. "*Mördervogel*? In the *DRS* laboratory?! Balloony, baloney," Bazcjk said. "Belahg, get your phone out," Blulip requested. They crowded around the smartphone's screen. The footage depicted post-mortem Colt. However, the soundtrack substantiated Blulip and Belahg's allegations to an extent. A rapid staccato, low frequency range, was distorting the smartphone's speaker. "Ok, I see." Rocket Bazcjk admitted that the death would have to be treated as suspicious. "P.I. Belahg! Find her. Bring me the *Mördervogel*," Bazcjk cried. Ok, P.I. Belahg said. Let's start by calling Hilary. P.I. Belahg suggested they call Hilary Park. Who do you call in the event of a pet casualty? A death in the extended family? Hilary Park from , of course. Hilary would PetCycle Colt. Also, Hilary would investigate whether Icy Pet, Loplop, or *Mördervogel* were still in the vicinity. Hilary would support bereft Rocket Bazcjk. *Hilfe*, Hilary. Hilary, help. That instant, they heard a crash that originated in Bobák/ Bazcjk's laboratory in the back of the *Dental Repair Shop*. Bazcjk picked up the phone all the more swiftly.

Half an hour later, Hilary arrived wearing her own *Helper Cell* T-shirt. Hilaire!! Hi. How can I help? Please take a seat in the waiting room. The longer Blulip's account continued, the clearer it became that it was affecting Hilary in unexpected ways. It was jinxing Hilary's usual swagger. It was interfering with her butch bravado. "Let me explain," Hilary said once Blulip had finished. Allegedly, a *Mördervogel*-like micro-Ewe had contaminated Contamino Park. Hilary Park corroborated Blulip's report, stating that, inexplicably, a feral *Vogel* had been *vor Ort*, contaminating the Contamino Park exhibition. Days ago, at PET CYCLE HO,

Holborn. "What you mean, '*Mördervogel*-like micro-Ewe'." "I know." Hilary understood the unlikelihood of a *Mördervogel*-like micro-Ewe contaminating HO. She was the first to admit the improbability. That's why Hilary had kept her *Mördervogel* visitation to herself. That's why Hilary had not even told Rocket Bazcjk. She had thought she had imagined things. She had thought she had lost it, gone soft in the head. Now, Hilary thought about Tracey B. Lulip, P.I. Belahg, Rocket Bazcjk, Icy Pet and the peony world they had in common. The pink-brown-and-coffee-cream polyester reality she had entered when entering the waiting room rendered multiple tentacles, balloony *Griffel, et cetera,* incredibly credible, promoting the plausibility of a *Mördervogel* going round South/central London. As far as Hilary was concerned, the pink-brown-and-coffee-cream poly-reality she shared with Tracey B. Lulip, P.I. Belahg, Rocket Bazcjk, and Icy Pet credibly furnished her own chimera with multiple tentacles, balloony *Griffel,* the whole shebang, and rendered the scenario of a serial *Mördervogel* going round London far more realistic than a psychotic hallucination affecting her personal faculties. By the first light of dawn, Hilary Park and Rocket Bazcjk entered the laboratory together. Prepared for the worst, they found the animal model's remains in a pool on the floor. No trace of Mv.

THE AQUA-*BLEU* MODEL

Shoulder-to-shoulder budgerigar statuettes extended along the workbench like a biological development study. All models were variations on a prototype, an oval torso supporting a globular head. Levels of intricacy varied, height, also colour. At 46 centimetres one of the larger specimens, the penultimate statuette in the series was painted in top-to-toe aqua-blue. She had no refined features bar a facial mark that hung from her mouth tongue-like and purple. A recent addition, the penultimate statuette was an updated model of P.I. Belahg's research object, Tulep. "She doesn't look right in the head," Belahg figured, meaning 'her head doesn't look right'. Why? Why didn't the penultimate statuette look right in the head? The aqua-*bleu* figurine was a representational flop. Far too literally did she incorporate recent evidence into a representation of Tulep. Her head was an *echinoidea*-inspired, spinesless endoskeleton, otherwise known as the 'hard test' of an urchin. P.I. Belahg had carved intricate ambulacral grooves and tubercles into the test, producing the varicose-veined, goose-bumped and featureless head in question. Matters had further deteriorated with the addition of the purple tongue. Ultimately, the penultimate statuette had failed the most basic test: the initial screen test. The camera had not loved her. Belahg loved her. But the camera had not. As a consequence, Director-General Blulip had a problem with her. And Belahg had a probem child on her hands.

Let's call the problem child 'Beau'. P.I. Belahg biroed a pedantic zigzag across Beau, producing a bedhead effect rather than *echinoidesque* spines, say, or budgerigarian plume. Better, Blulip? Can Beau go on TV? No way. *Die kommt mir nicht ins Fernsehen.* P.I. Belahg put Beau back on the shelf, sandwiching her between the antepenultimate and ultimate budgerigar models. Maintaining her position as the ultimate model in the series, Healthy-lips remained the one to be beaten.

But Healthy-lips did look a bit dated now. Despite her reservations, P.I. Belahg decided that, henceforth, Beau would supercede Healthy-lips as her primary investigative lead. (P.I. Belahg really did love problem child Beau.) Ok, Blulip said, but not female lead. Blulip reiterated that under no circumstances would Beau work as the female, male, or transgender lead in her digi TV show. Ok, Belahg said. Don't listen to her, Belahg whispered into Beau's ear. Beau didn't listen. Ok, good night, Blulip. P.I. Belahg took herself off to bed early. Blulip stayed up working late.

PAINLEVÉ HYPERCAMP

A supermoon pink-flooded the workshop on Harpur Street and all things therein. An ebay-bought second-hand digicam and an ex-professional camera dolly had appeared in the workshop. Belahg was sleeping on the floor alongside the kitchenette. Blulip was having a go at editing their recent footage. She was having a go at making the footage work for Tulep.tv. A neo-scientific drama failed to unfold on the laptop screen. A poetic experiment perhaps, with a camp ethos, conducted under a rarer, queerer star, but not the future blockbuster Blulip had hoped for. The pressure to follow their breakthrough *4th Episode,* 'Peggy Shaw and Lois Weaver (*Split Britches*) cruise Hilary Park (PET CYCLE)', and the Transgender Arabesque's premonition of Tulep.tv's going under, were impacting on Blulip's production of the *5th Episode.* These pressures were taking their toll on Blulip's editorial panache and natural bravado.

A knock on the door. It was P.I. Belagh's rival, P.I. Loveday from Holborn Detectives PLC. Hi. Long time, no see. P.I. Loveday was paying Blulip an unwelcome late night visit. May I come in? P.I. Loveday asked. Not really, Blulip replied. Blulip said she was editing Tulep.tv's *5th Episode.* Ah! Let's have a look. P.I. Loveday let herself in. She pulled over a chair and sat down next to Blulip.

What on earth, P.I. Loveday said.

A close up of an aquarium animal, sure, but where was the action in that? Jacques Cousteau's *Night of the Squid* sprang to mind as a superior example of the genre, or perhaps Jean Painlevé's *Les Assassins d'Eau Douce* (1949), *Freshwater Assassins.* With Genevieve Hamon, *haute-bourgeois* avant-gardener Jean Painlevé had been pioneering surrealist science-films such as *Les Assassins d'Eau Douce, Les Danseuses de la Mar* (1956), and, significantly, the anticipatory betterment of Blulip's *5th Episode*, *Les Oursins* (1954), Engl.: *Sea Urchins.* Watching a Youtube version, Loveday felt that *Les Oursins* handsdown outperformed

Blulip's *5th Episode*, if not in terms of poetics, in terms of action and drama. Further, P.I. Loveday contended, *Les Oursins* had been shot in '54, sixty-odd years before the *5th Episode*. Loveday wanted to know what this, the *5th Episode*, added to the existing attempt. How was it new? A minute and a half into the video for example, Painlevé and Hamon's animal star was seen agitating the ocean-floor by way of bodily micro-movements, or corporal wiggling. Look. The capture informed Loveday and Blulip that *l'oursin* was digesting: "*L'intestine est donc bourre de sable et en digere les particules nutritives.*" Compare that, Painlevé and Hamon's self-sufficient, sand-churning, submarine mini-hydrofoil, to Blulip's inanimate Colt. Following the close-up of *l'oursin* absorbing *la nutrition*, the French film cut to a scientist's hand live-dissecting the mini-hydrofoil with a small pair of scissors. The scientist opened her up along the length of her abdomen so as to showcase for the camera *son intestine,* now indigesting. In the right hand column of the screen, Youtube recommended a clip, *How to Eat Sea Urchin*. Unlike the *5th Episode*, P.I. Loveday continued, *Les Oursins* had advanced 'neo-zoological drama' in significant ways. *Neo-zoological Drama* had been a concept developed by Jean Painlevé in the pseudoscientific, hoax text of the same name, which he had submitted to *l'Académie des Sciences* in '29. Given these high calibre precedents, Loveday insisted, it was not a moment too soon that Blulip stopped and reflected and asked herself what constituted drama today. "What constitutes drama today?!" Loveday insinuated that the future of Tulep.tv depended on these and similar questions. "Audiences love drama," Loveday declared. As well as *Les Oursins,* the French *haute-bourgois* dramaturges had produced *Cristaux Liquides* (1978), and a film showing a male sea horse in labour pain, *L'Hippocampe* (1939). *L'Hippocampe,* Hypercamp. Painlevé Hypercamp just popped into existence. Shadow of her future self at this stage, Painlevé Hypercamp would become Blulip's future drag alter ego. Blulip did not tell P.I. Loveday about Painlevé Hypercamp. For now, Blulip kept Hypercamp to herself. Blulip put Hypercamp on the backburner for now.

P.I. Loveday, meanwhile, was on a roll, debating the future of drama in terms of its past. Come to think of it. Loveday came to think of it. What had been the public reception of *Cristaux Liquides*, or *L'Hippocampe*? Fanatic, but marginal. The films had incited isolated instances of fanaticism, but they had not attained widespread popularity. Here's another example, Loveday continued. Forget the French. Neo-scientific drama was taken to the next level by Austrian nationals, of all people.

Like the better-known Jacques Cousteau, Austrian *Unterwasserfotograf, Tauchpionier, Meeresbiologe*, and *Patriarch* Hans Hass (1919-2013) had extended Painlevé and Hamon's early concept of neo-zoological drama, producing neo-scientific blockbusters. *MENSCHEN UNTER HAIEN* (1947, 84 Min.), for example. *MENSCHEN UNTER HAIEN* featured an early-development underwater breathing apparatus that in one instance had caused Hass's onscreen oxygen intoxication. The crucial transformation from documentary into feature film, *Kassenschlager, mit Millionenpublikum*, had been attributed to the contribution of Lotte Hass, Loveday said. Secretary, underwater fotographer, underwater glamour model and actor, Lotte had outperformed Hans's sharks on a regular basis. *Sie stahl jedem Hai die Show.* Née Baierl, the media were quick to rename her Lotte *Haierl.* Lotte Little-Shark. Charisma and showmanship had transformed underwater poetics into box office hits, and that was the sort of drama Blulip should develop Tulep.tv according to. Put a human actor-amongst! Give the audience a way in. The presence of a shark lady, for example, mitigated the fundamental alienness of a baby-seal killing predator. Go further. Anthropomorph your monsters. Call your sharks Mr. Shark [sic]! Make them relevant to your viewers. Meanwhile, proliferating aquatic scenarios conjured another one still. Blulip half-remembered an Argentinian/French short story from the 1950s, *Axolotl,* that featured the eponymous Mexican walking fish. The axolotl's utmost otherness was the precise quality that the story's narrator recognised and connected with, despite the absence of Lotte Hass or any other interspecies intermediaries. "Anthropogenic!" P.I. Loveday exclaimed, disrupting Blulip's reverie. "More importantly: Photogenic! If in doubt, provide EYE CANDY," Loveday advised. "I leave it with you." And with these words, P.I. Loveday left.

Left alone, Blulip contemplated what she would come to think of as *Loveday's brief.* The pink supermoon, perhaps, and her wish to repeat Tulep.tv's recent success had rendered her strangely susceptible to Loveday's influence, *Loveday's brief.* That was despite Loveday being a rogue agent that Blulip herself (regretted she) had (ever) recruited.

Blulip began manufacturing a version of a bikini from the previously inconsequential theatre backcloth depicting 'day'. Blulip sewed a daylight delight, a nifty bikini. There was no women's underwear in Blulip and Belahg's shared household that could be adapted. Not really, only already appropriated men's pants and *Bjorn Borg*™ hybrids for gender activists. However, *Loveday's brief,* Blulip's agenda w/r/t Tulep.tv, overlapping subaqueous scenarios, and specifically Lotte Hass and the short story *Axolotl,* coalesced to engender a figure that required a nifty kit, a bikini outfit. Introducing: AxoLottl, the character, the audience attractor, the aberration. The eye-catching bikini-wearer, EYE CANDY, and Tulep.tv's next star and agitator. In the small hours, Blulip fabricated AxoLottl's bikini. Finally, it was done.

"Belahg, put some clothes on," Blulip said. "Put these clothes on."

Belahg rose. She was wearing a large soft-cotton T-shirt and large men's underpants. Blulip strapped the new digital camera to the professional tripod dolly. Then she addressed Belahg, priming her, calling out: "AxoLottl!" Blulip handed 'AxoLottl' the bikini bottoms she had sewn. Still half asleep, AxoLottl (Belahg) put on the bikini bottoms over, repeat: OVER, her men's pants. Next, Blulip handed AxoLottl the bikini top she had sewn. AxoLottl put on the bikini top over, rpt: OVER, her oversize T-shirt. "Supra," Blulip approved. Next, Blulip produced a cubit-long, aqua-*bleu* budgerigar figurine. The cubit-long, aqua-*bleu* budgerigar figurine was THEE inhuman(e) object, THEE *objet de* concern, that AxoLottl was to render palatable, attractive and relevant to an otherwise indifferent audience. Blulip's budgerigar figurine was Hans Hass's shark, Jean Painlevé 's *oursin,* and representative of anything that was likely to feature heavily in Tulep.tv's subsequent programming. Anthropomorph the monster, Blulip recalled *Loveday's brief.* Anthropomorph the cubit-long, inhuman(e) *objet de,* by sheer anthropo-proximity. Using gaffer tape, Blulip proceeded to strap *l'objet de* concern, the aqua-*bleu* budgerigar figurine, vertically to AxoLottl's right thigh. Producing anthropo-proximity, Blulip strapped *l'objet de* concern lengthwise to AxoLottl's right thigh. Then Blulip retreated. Operation 'AxoLottl! Anthropomorph *l'objet*!' was operative. It was all systems go. The digi-cam was recording. From here on, AxoLottl was meant to extemporise. The idea was for her to enact a mutual connection between *l'objet* and the AxoLottl character, so as to transform *l'objet,* AxoLottl, the lot, into something with a lot of public appeal. The strategy backfired. For starters, AxoLottl was not as at ease in her bikini as Lotte Hass might have been. Supra or not, AxoLottl was not. AxoLottl blew her top the moment she became half-aware of what she was wearing. She went ballistic. Not for nothing had she, Belahg, b.1974, spent 1975-201x rejecting the bog-standard femininity epitomised in the item of clothing she found herself wearing. (Try putting a butch in a bikini.) Not for nothing had she, Belahg, spent 1975 to today rejecting the bog-standard, bikini-sporting, frock-donning femininity enforced by an autobiographical family, autobiographical paediatricians, autobiographical teachers, autobiographical schoolchildren, and an autobiographical public, in order of vehemence. At significant personal cost, Belahg had not gone near a bikini in living memory. There existed photographs of a ten-year-old in a variety of ill-fitting suits and incongruous cravats. A series of abortive hair-do and hair-dye experiments, 1981-1990, were archived photographically, epitomising the coming-of-age related crisis experienced specifically by the genderqueer teenager. Do not say that EVERY teenage is critical. Look at the photos. Ebony Black. Night Blue Black. BlackViolet Black. Blackest Black. And, godhelpus, Auburn. Blond highlights in Ebony Black, starched-collar white shirt, black skinny necktie, and black pleated trousers, and that's just one of the more coherent attempts at a look: a ten-year-old's D.I.Y. wildgirl interpretation of Simon Le Bon. In 1984, any wildgirl incarnation of Simon Le Bon would have been enough… to... In 1984, Simone Le Bon had caused consternation in hinterland Europe. Subsequently, the eleven, twelve, thirteen-year-old had failed to grow out of it. It had gone on for too long. They had conspired to fuck *die Faxen* out of the child. By tacit agreement, the gender police had seen to the dyke child being taught many life lessons. Lest she become a bulldagger. Lest she become a fully-fledged, raving, raging, reckoning and incorrigible adult powerdagger. Strong and unhinged. What if she organised. Already there had been *Techtelmechtel* with that wildgirl interpretation of John Taylor. Girl-on-girl hanky-panky. Innocent, but. Best nipped in the bud.

Reliving her childhood, AxoLottl was having a meltdown. The bikini had triggered a critical flashback. Anxious to remove her contraptions, AxoLottl was yanking the budgerigar figurine strapped to her thigh. Blulip did a double take. A tiny pink LED was signalling that the digicam was recording. AxoLottl was struggling with extrastrong gaffer tape, crying *schlosshund*-like. Oh dear, Blulip thought. Experiment 'AxoLottl! Anthropomorph *l'objet*!' was spiralling out of control. The scene's unexpectedly risqué but not unattractive quality was being undermined by the high levels of personal distress on display. Experiment AxoLottl was, if not failing, derailing. AxoLottl was alienating future audiences the way she was having a meltdown. Not a minute too soon did Blulip realise that only one person could save the day and that was Painlevé Hypercamp. Personification of a post-adolescent context shaped by decades on the queer scene, Painlevé Hypercamp was to restore the perspective of a seasoned gay. Rather than *Maman* or *Papa* Belahg, Painlevé Hypercamp was to provide the context in which a bikini on a butch meant genderqueer camp rather than normative femininity. In short, Painlevé Hypercamp was to re-establish the abnormality that they inhabited day in day out, and that temporarily seemed to have disappeared in an autobiographical time-warp. Pressed to save the day *subito,* Painlevé Hypercamp, when it came to it, was just Blulip with her top off, engaging in hypocamp micromovement. Hypocamp micromovement was a strangely microfied, butoh-like, and restrained full-body expression of gay exuberance. In this way, Painlevé Hypercamp microadvanced towards AxoLottl, wildgirl John-Taylor-like. AxoLottl ceased having a psychotrip promptly. AxoLottl returned from her psychojourney *prontamente.* Painlevé Hypercamp and AxoLottl proceeded to hypocamp in a most consolatory fashion. They made moves to remove Axo's contraption, the aqua-*bleu objet de* concern. The digicam was recording. Eventually, gaffer gave way. When it came to it, AxoLottl prevented Painlevé Hypercamp from removing her suprabikini. AxoLottl said that the rescue operation had been accomplished, and that no further actions would be required. Thank you, Painlevé. Pleasure. Relaxing into her character and her suprabikini, AxoLottl microdanced with Painlevé Hypercamp into a low-battery indicator LED sunset.

Eventually the camera turned itself off. Ding, the doorbell went. P.I. Belahg and Blulip disbanded. Blulip opened the door. The great Belua entered the workshop. Belua hesitated, looking questioningly from Blulip to Belahg. "Is this a bad time?" Belua asked. "To the contrary," Blulip responded.

BELUA

Belua was a broad-shouldered quadruped with a disproportionately small, pastel-blue head. Belua was a large and rectangular quadruped with one pronounced collarbone. Belua could barely fit through the door. She made her entrance lengthwise, left shoulder first. Who are you? Belahg asked, projecting her question upwards and towards Belua's small head. The head was pastel-blue and budgerigar-shaped. The head perched on a hypertrophied, pink-brown-and-coffee-cream-coloured collarbone. Belua was a composite character consisting of two human characters, the rolled up carpet they carried, and an errant bird perching on it. The carpet roll that connected the humans played the role of the pink-brown-and-coffee-cream-coloured collarbone of the brand-new beastie. Hello, Belua! Whilst waiting to hear from the head, Belahg changed from her suprabikini into something more decent. Belahg swapped her bikini for her Y-3 *Hero* joggers. She put her *adidas* trainers on. Who are you, and, in respect to recent debauchery, what are you? *Sittenpolizei? Sittichpolizei?* The vice squad? A turquoise tumour hung from Belua's head's, what, lower eyelid. A bright turquoise tumour emblazoned the head's eyelid. Some form of Abrikossof's? Or a stye? Belua's head detached from her broad-shouldered body and volplaned onto the workbench. The head ran past a row of turpentine bottles and hid behind a pot of paint. Belua apologised for the late night visitation. Headless, she spoke from the heart. Belua proceeded further to disintegrate. Her shoulder duplex disengaged from her collarbone. The latter landed on the floor. Finally, Belua's broad torso bifurcated, and Belua was gone. *Sapperlot!* Hilary, Bobák, it's you, it's you! Hilary Park and Rocky Bobák were wearing their *Helper Cell* T-shirts. They had thick streaks of glitter down their cheeks like some kind of war paint. They had come to the workshop as Belua, and with an agenda.

They wanted to Combat A Localised Evil. They

wanted to Combat A Localised Evil, who was wreaking havoc across SW2 and WC1X. They were to bring down the *Mördervogel*, A Localised Evil. They were to repurpose existing microinfrastructures such as Tulep.tv to support the manhunt. Extending a tradition of radical media activism (think *Born in Flames* (1983), think *ACT UP* media strategies), they were to repurpose existing microinfrastructures and issue a public appeal. They were to issue *einen Fahndungsaufruf* on Tulep.tv.

Hilary Park explained how, earlier, Rocky Bobák had come to see her at PET CYCLE HO on the Gray's Inn Road. Initially, Park and Bobák had intended to broadcast a video-version of a mug shot, a moving wanted-poster, so to speak. They had intended to televise a digitally animated reconstruction of the fugitive *Mördervogel*. Do you recognise this, or one similar? Do you recognise anything on the basis of this? Would anyone who knows anything please come forward? In order to create an identikit composite of the missing subject, Hilary and Bobák had employed SketchCop-FACETTE, FACES 2000, and/or the latest EvoFit or EFIT-V softwares, whose algorithms are based on evolutionary mechanisms. Park and Bobák had spent the afternoon on SketchCop-FACETTE. ("Click, capture, convict.") It had transpired that the Mv's facette was not capturable. The Mv's facette was not reconstructable via the regular technologies. SketchCop-FACETTE's algorithms had failed to generate a likely facial composition. By their own admission, Hilary and Bobák had struggled to input reliable data. They had failed to select – 'click' – appropriate facial components. SketchCop-FACETTE's database of facial components had offered nothing that had approximated the *Mördervogel*'s redeye, for example... "Red?!" Bobák had cried, "purple!" ...nor the *Mördervogel*'s typical pinklip. "What pink lips you have, birdie." After hours of compiling e-collage faces, Hilary Park and Rocky Bobák had concluded that SketchCop-FACETTE was not going to be the technology that would bring the Great British public their *Mördervogel*. Nor was it going to jog their own memory, sketchy at best. Was *Mördervogel* inch-high and bloated? Balloony, baloney, or Loplop-like? Blue-faced or green-headed? The reconstruction of the *Mördervogel* called for another strategy.

This afternoon at HO, Hilary and Bobák had asked themselves where else to begin. Where else to begin? Where better to begin than before the beginning. Hilary Park and Rocky Bobák had decided to conduct a more thorough reconstruction of the elusive character. For starters, the *Mördervogel* was a progeny of the Icy Pet, aka ICI PET of the peony-sewerduct-lizardine lineage. A triple-barrelled dynasty whose formative influence on the *Mördervogel* was impossible to ignore. Any effective reconstructive attempt would be based on the pink-brown-and-coffee-cream polyester reality that harboured the Icy Pet, and that in conjunction with Hilary, Blulip and Belahg's respective real-life encounters with T★★★p had given shape to the *Mördervogel* that night in the *DRS* waiting-room. "Let's take a trip South." Park and Bobák had driven the former's *Suzuki Alto*, via Waterloo Bridge and the Elephant & Castle, towards Streatham. They had parked the *Alto* on Brixton Hill. They had entered the *Dental Repair Shop ___k_ ___ák*, or ______ *___air _hop ___k_ ___ák*. The carpet was there on the waiting-room floor. Hello, English Heritage Grade II listed *Prunkstück*. Home to many a living thing, including the Icy Pet. "Carpets are botanical and zoological parks," J. Tierno Jr., Ph.D., microbiologist, immunologist and author of *The Secret Life of Germs*, once said to *Men's Health*. Hilary Park and Rocky Bobák had taken up the carpet. They had rolled it up, shouldered it, and carried it out of the door. They had strapped it to the roof of the *Alto*. Hilary and Bobák had returned to Holborn via the Elephant & Castle and Tower Bridge. They had parked outside HO. They had shouldered and carried the carpet roll down the Theobald's Road towards Blulip's on Harpur Street. In transit, they had attracted a feathered friend. The feathered friend had settled on the carpet roll/collarbone, completing Belua. They had rolled up at Blulip's as Belua.

Hilary unfurled the infamous carpet on the workshop's floor. "Plan B depends on teamwork," Hilary explained. Team 'Reconstruct *Mördervogel*', or Team Reco.*Mö*, includes you, you, you, and the Icy Pet. The Icy Pet's participation was crucial, Hilary said. One could not extrapolate *Mördervogel* from a non-participant Icy Pet. No Icy Pet, no Mv. Ah, ok, Blulip said. Let's try it. You on? You're on! Hilary Park, Rocky Bobák, P.I. Belahg and Tracey B. Lulip gathered on the waiting-room carpet, now in the workshop, banking on its germinal properties. Peony, peony, lizardine sewer-duct. Wait. How did it go again? Peony, peony, lizardine travesty. Pink-brown-and-coffee-cream polyculiarity? Something like that. Eventually, a vague presence made herself felt. Not prominently, but. Competing against an array of peony variations, lizardine sewer-ducts, and botanico-zoological biodiversities, Icy Pet made a reluctant entrance. From many plural realities, the relevant Icy Pet eventually rose. Team Reco.*Mö* was good to go.

They tried a couple of tested techniques to get the reconstruction of the *Mördervogel* off the ground. Specifically, they tried parlour games (like Exquisite Corpse). Blulip introduced an A4 sheet of paper and a biro. On the upper eighth of the sheet, Blulip biroed an olivey shape from which two short dashes descended like the outline of a neck or the legs of a bird. Leaving half an inch of the connection lines visible, Blulip folded the top of the sheet over her contribution. Next, Belahg's turn. Belahg diverted the vertical connection lines horizontally outwards, producing an almighty collarbone.

What were they thinking?

The reconstruction of the Mv on the basis of Icy Pet was blighted by the fact that, in transit, Icy Pet had taken on *another* life of her own. A life other than *Mördervogel*. Via the pink-brown-and-coffee-cream carpet-come-collarbone, with rubber underlay, Icy Pet in conjunction with Hilary, Bobák and the currently undertheorised feathered friend, had given rise to another spook, namely the *Mördervogel*'s successor/variant/overlord, Überbestie Belua. The *Mördervogel*'s broadshouldered, small-headed brothersister was affecting the ongoing reconstructive effort. Unless *Mördervogel* was unusually Belua-like, and had a collarbone to die for, for example. Unless *Mördervogel* had cephalic atrophy, featherbrain, birdbrain. Unless *Mördervogel* had either of these, Überbest*ie* Belua was affecting the ongoing *Mördervogel* reconstruction significantly and in the wrong way.

Lately, P.I. Belahg, Tracey Blulip, Rocky Bobák and Hilary Park had started to question the ongoing groundswell of crackpot a[n]ge[l](nt)s. Wherever they looked, ≈Δ≈ had been proliferating at breakneck speed. They could no longer tell whether they were coming or going. They had better start killing some of them off. Keep them in check. It was unsafe to invent too many angels (Spicer, J., *The Unvert Manifesto,* 1954). They ended up ruling the roost. Already, Team Reco.*Mö* were committed to overthrowing the *Mördervogel.* They were in the process of taking the *Mörder*≈Δ≈ down. They should have started, however, with crackpot Belua. If only they hadn't lost track of Belua. They let Belua slip through the net.

P.I. Belahg folded the already folded part of the paper over her contribution and passed it on. Next, Hilary's turn. Hilary concentrated on the micro-Ewe who had contaminated Contamino Park, and whom she had brought in connection with the *Mördervogel* that night in the *DRS* waiting-room. Then Hilary let the biro do its thing. *Huch!* Had Hilary let *Belua* do her thing?! Was this Belua's handiwork? A Belua/biro conspiracy?! A nondescript thorax emerged, two verticals descending from the almighty collarbone. Hilary folded and passed on the shrinking A4 sheet. She got up and fetched four bottles of *KHelp*™ from the Blulip's mini-*Fridgette.*

Bobák's turn next. The vocable 'HELP', capital letters, rang in her head. Bobák was the character with chronic health difficulties. One of her kidneys was failing. No one but Hilary knew. This was Bobák's immune system beseeching *angelus* Icy Pet. help, Icy Pet, HELP. The biro fell short of channelling the complex event. Bobák ended up merely extending Hilary's verticals, engendering a generic midriff on paper. Oh dear.

Next, Blulip's turn. What if Blulip was wearing her *Christopher Ala* shark-print T-shirt. What if hundreds of sharks were playing along. What if, for Blulip, *KHelp*™ evoked Colt. What if *KHelp*™ evoked Diamond-Jaws Colt, Tiger-like Colt, Shark-Prowess Colt, Prior-to-being-murdered-by-*Mördervogel* Colt? What if, for Blulip, *KHelp*™ evoked Hooked-onto-Nigel Colt, Killer-Appetite Colt, Kelp-Overdose Colt? (What if, inadvertently, kelp, or Nigel!?, had killed Colt?!) Channelling Colt, Blulip drew like a person possessed. Blulip wielded the biro. Her jaw muscles tensed. Blulip produced a magnificent row of cuspidate teeth. Blulip biroed four magnified fangs across the remaining half of the sheet. Like this: VVVV. In *lieu* of, say, lower extremities. One might have expected the lower extremities of their Exquisite Corpse there. VVVV's cusps toed the terminal edge of the A4 sheet of paper. Game over, Hilary said. Unfolding the sheet, Belahg unveiled the group's concerted efforts at capturing the *Mördervogel*. A sketch emerged of small-headed, broad-shouldered and four-legged Belua.

BIKINI ATOLL

Pre-Bikini Atoll was a 12-year-old from West Croydon. Pre-Bikini Atoll preferred the gender neutral pronouns 'they'/'them', but 'she'/'her' were ok, too. Watching Painlevé Hypercamp and AxoLottl on Tulep.tv (the *6th Episode*), Pre-Bikini's world (West Croydon) changed forever. They would not share the relevant link round their social networks and forget about it. Instead, they would act upon the *6th Episode* in significant ways and over a sustained period of time. Over the next 7/8 years, Pre-Bikini would develop AxoLottl's choleric tendencies for comic effect, and into the fully fleshed-out, multi-media persona Bikini Atoll. Pre-Bikini's future act would combine Pro-People Protest and Socialist Striptease. Bikini Atoll would perform a Micronesian Demon Girl character, for example, haunting cardboard cutouts of US colonisers. The cardboard cutout of US colonisers would stand in for imperialists worldwide, and across history. By the time they were 18, Bikini Atoll would hold a residency not at the RVT (Royal Vauxhall Tavern), nor at The Glory in Faggerston, but with a *nouveau*-anarcho cabaret troupe called 'The Avant-garde of the Oppressed'. 'The Avant-garde of the Oppressed' would perform predominately around Penge and Surbiton.

DEADWOOD-TO-DYNAMO

Belua's head had been living at Blulip's for weeks now. The head resided behind a pot of paint. In spite of her bright turquoise tumour, the head seemed fine. She bounded across the workbench like an ebullient micro-stallion. The head left footprints all over the workbench. She left footprints all over the Exquisite Corpse. Her tracks were shaped like 1.5 cm ø horseshoes. They were the tracks of a mini-filly. The head's tracks were shaped like 1.5 cm ø kidneys, slightly contracting. Maroon-coloured kidneys, a little too crooked and too tightly puckered up for their own good. They littered the workbench and Team Reco.*Mö*'s concertinaed *Cadavre Exquis.* Tonight was a big night for Team Reco.*Mö*. Tracey B. Lulip, P.I. Belahg, Hilary Park and Rocky Bobák had gathered at Blulip's to televise live their *Cadavre Exquis.* This was the mugshot they had extrapolated for televisual purposes. For better or worse, the mugshot depicted Überbestie Belua. From 8.15pm, Tulep.tv's first Saturday night transmission was to go live. The show would adapt a BOLO (Be On the Look-Out) or ATL (Attempt To Locate) format. The show would adapt a format that was being referred to as BOLO (Be On the Look-Out) or ATL (Attempt To Locate), in shop language. Their angels had been proliferating at breakneck speed and they needed containing. There were so many of them now. They no longer knew whether they were coming or going. Team Reco.*Mö* had spent weeks Combating A Localised Evil, for example. They had been trying to take out the *Mördervogel.* But Combating A Localised Evil, if anything, had fuelled the invigoration of deadwood. Not that this, the *Cadavre Exquis*, was the face of localised evil. This was Belua. Belua was just another adrenalysed angel interfering with events. Belua was just another crackpot ≈Δ≈ that a cooperative public should Be On the Look-Out for. That a cooperative public should BOLO (Be On the Look-Out) for, ATL (Attempt To Locate), and HD, help deactivate. Render inoperative.

Live punditry would be provided by Hilary Park and Rocky Bobák. Co-pundit Park was wearing her *Helper Cell* T-shirt and rolled up chinos. She was wearing her *Nasir Mazhar* cap with high-camp side pencil holder. Employing the workbench as a makeshift dressing room table, Bobák and Hilary helped each other get ready. Bobák was touching up war-paint around Hilary's eyes and forehead. Co-pundit Bobák was wearing joggers, tennis socks and *adidas* trainers. *Oben,* Bobák was *ohne.* Bobák was *oben-ohne,* Bobák was topless. "Can we have the heating on in the television studio, please?" Hilary called. A fresh scar descended from Bobák's chest down her blue-hued abdomen. Rainbow coloured *haematomata* littered the area butterfly-like. Genitalia-shaped insects and worms bellied beneath Bobák's filigree ribcage. One too many kidneys bellied beneath Bobák's post-op ribcage. Three kidneys: two home-grown, one shop-bought. It was standard transplantation procedure to leave defunct kidneys in place, did you know that. How is a kidney transplant performed? According to *NHS Choices*, a left donor kidney is implanted on your right side; a right donor kidney is implanted on your left side. This facilitates ureter-to-urinary-bladder suturing, apparently. Copying the crescent shapes that covered the *Cadavre Exquis*, Hilary drew thick maroon lipstick across Bobák's colourful torso and face. Colonising Bobák's already colourful torso and face were 1.5 cm diameter kidney Nr. 4, 1.5 cm diameter kidney Nr. 5, 1.5 cm diameter kidney Nrs. 6, 7, 8. Hilary kept adding 1.5 cm diameter lipstick kidneys. 9, 10, for example. 11, 12. When she put down the *Manhattan Berry Baby*™ lipstick, an army of back-up organs, the size of a leech each, were colonising Bobák's already colourful torso and face. Like this, Rocky Bobák turned to the camera. Good evening. Good evening, global underbelly. Your host for the evening. "We're live," Blulip said. Co-pundits Bobák and Park framed the concertinaed mugshot, the *Cadavre Exquis* blu-tacked to the wall behind them.

"Do you or does anyone you know have any knowledge

of her or one similar," Hilary began. But rather than issue the BOLO, or the ATL. Rather than issue the BOLO (Be On the Look-Out), or the ATL (Attempt To Locate), and ask a cooperative public to participate in the containment of deadwood obstreperousness. Rather than issue the BOLO, or the ATL, Hilary Park stopped short. She was undergoing a change of mind, live. A significant *Sendepause* occurred. A radio silence. Seelonce, sehlawnce, *silenzio*. Flat airwaves. Hilary looked at her topless co-pundit. Bobák returned the look. Then Hilary put her left arm around Bobák's shoulders. And Bobák put her right arm around Hilary's shoulders. Doubling their chest girth, they began re(as)sembling the original fourlegger, the almighty Belua. Doubling their shoulder length, they effectively began re(as)sembling the original Belua. And rather than issue the BOLO, or the ATL, Belua performed a significant U-ey. Half-formed Belua performed *eine radikale Kehrtwendung*. A drastic U-turn. Belua's ideas re Saturday night entertainment departed significantly from both, the BOLO and ALT formats. Belua believed in freak proliferation. "Pro Dynamo Deadwood!" Belua bellowed. There can never be too many crackpot agents. Belua offered this half-formed wisdom, that there could never be too much hyperactive riffraff interfering with events. Pro Dynamo Deadwood. Pro for 'proliferate'. Now Bobák's fist flew up. Bobák agreed with Belua. There was nothing like backup. Already Bobák regretted their previous stance re the *Mördervogel*. Why do away with her? There was nothing like killer backup. Look at the rate at which we disintegrate, Bobák said. We need any support we might get. "In Scotland, *in vitro* production of human organs from stem cells has been making remarkable progress," Hilary said. Yes, Bobák had heard of this new research in Scotland, Socialist Britain. "Meanwhile, we are launching a competition," Belua told an uninitiated live audience. It just came out. "Instead of the advertised BOLO bulletin," Belua said, "we are presenting the Deadwood-to-Dynamo (?) Audience Prize." The prize, albeit brand-new, has many a patron already. Icy Pet is a patron of the Deadwood-to-Dynamo Prize. The GoldSeXUal StatuEtte is a patron of the Deadwood-to-Dynamo Audience Prize. Orsun Ursol is a patron of the Deadwood-to-Dynamo Audience Prize. Painlevé Hypercamp and AxoLottl are patrons of the Deadwood-to-Dynamo Audience Prize. The new UUs, Colt, Healthy-lips, the FtM/T legion, Peggy and the sharks are patron saints of the Deadwood-to-Dynamo Audience Prize. We are inviting a co-operative public to submit their propositions for a Tulep.tv Season Finale. Low budget productions of epic proportions, format discretionary. Anything legible eligible. Tulep.tv are looking for this season's finale, or the *8th Episode.* Accepting submissions now. Do the general public. Want to add. Riffraff. Add your riffraff to ours. There can never be too many madcap angels on Tulep.tv. Belua brandished her Herculean chest. Forget Atl, forget Bolo. Who, for example, was A-Bolo-tl? Co-operative public, we are asking you, bring us Abolotl! The willy-nilly invention of ≈Δ≈ might carry significant risks. But it is unsafer not to invent ANY angels. It is entirely unsafe to uninvent angels. This is what we think at Tulep.tv. What do YOU think?!

Cut, camera operator Blulip said.

P.I. Belahg on the laptop switched to adverts, a 10 seconds ad of Hilary Park enjoying a glass of *KHelp*™. Then a non-transmission period ensued. Team 'Resu.*Mö*' (Team 'Resurrect *Mördervogel*') looked at each other. Okeh. Ok? Ohki. Deadwood-to-Dynamo?! Season Finale?! Ok then. Everyone liked the idea. It had just come out like that, but everyone liked the idea. Half-formed Belua disbanded.

EINE GANZ VORZÜGLICHE LEICHE, UN CADAVRE EXQUIS, AND BELOVED

Out of hold, rainbow-coloured Rocky Bobák disappeared against the paint splattered workbench. Without Hilary's support, Bobák approximated a corpse rather than anything more exquisite. You know how Freddy Mercury appeared in *The Show Must Go On* (1991) video? Hilary handed Bobák a *Helper Cell* T-shirt. It was 10 days since Bobák's transplantation. But for Hilary, the lipstick marks on Bobák's body evoked not the recent past, but two distant pasts. 1872 and 1991. Moritz Kaposi, Hungarian Dermatologist, on the one hand. And *eine ganz vorzügliche Leiche, un Cadavre Exquis,* and beloved, on the other. For Hilary, the *Berry Baby*™ marks on Bobák's body evoked the past, 1872, on the one hand. Originally described by Moritz Kaposi, Hungarian Dermatologist, Kaposi's sarcoma is caused by herpesvirus 8 (HHV8). Kaposi's sarcoma (KS) is a systemic disease that presents with cutaneous lesions. In the 1980s, KS became known as an AIDS-related illness, AIDS being an acronym for Acquired Immune Deficiency Syndrome. On the grounds of its noticability and depictability, KS became *the* AIDS-defining symptom. Herpesvirus 8 (HHV8) is one of 7 known concoviruses. HHV8 is transmitted by organ transplantation or very deep kissing. For Hilary, the *Berry Baby*™ marks on Bobák's body merged two distinct pasts, 1872 and 1991, and fetched them into the present. In 1991, 17-year-old Hilary's 41-year-old uncle had died of pneumonia within 40 days of his diagnosis with HIV. Hilary's uncle had not left the hospital after his diagnosis with Human Immunodeficiency Virus infection (HIV). For 30 of 40 days he had been articially respirated. For 30 of 40 days he had died on life support. Within 40 days of his diagnosis with HIV, Hilary's uncle had died. On the other hand, Hilary's uncle's 36-year-old boyfriend had survived without wanting to. After Hilary's uncle's death, Hilary's uncle's partner had lived on to buy every available book on the subject of 'Life in the Afterlife', 'Afterlife Communication (16 Proven Methods)', 'Engaging Descriptions of the Afterlife from Someone Living There', 'The Afterlife is as Real as This Life', and 'Your Eternal Self' (in English). During this period (after life), Hilary had founded the *Helper Cell* action group. *Helper Cell* had been an attempt to de-individualise AIDS, and a subdivision of more global forms of AIDS-related activism, for example *ACT UP (AIDS Coalition to Unleash Power).* In '91, in rural South Korea, *Helper Cell* had been a one member action group. For most of its history, *Helper Cell* had been a cell of one. For most of its history, *Helper Cell*, as an action cell, had failed to achieve its objectives. As an initiative, it had fallen flat on its face. *Helper Cell* had helped no one. Today, *Helper Cell* was an LQBTQI action group with pent-up activist potential. For Hilary, the marks on Bobák's torso and face evoked Kaposi's sarcoma (KS), Freddy Mercury, and *un cadavre* extremely beloved. But Bobák's marks were tiny reinforcement organs. They were make-up renal machines. With lipstick kidney support, Rocky Bobák had been convalescing from surgery. This was not the past, neither 1872, nor 1991. This was 201x, and the *Helper Cell* Ts were working.

SEASON FINALE

Look at it. Without its negligible head, the *Cadavre Exquis* resembled a Maxillary Molar. Without its already negligible head, the *Cadavre Exquis*'s bulbous body and VVVV extremities approximated a 4-canal Maxillary Molar. Without its silly Belua-head, the Exquisite Corpse resembled a toxic tulip. Toxic Tulep?! No, tulip. A topsy-turvy toxic tulip. Headless, the *Cadavre Exquis* looked like Orsun Ursol. Hello Orsun, you friendly, genderqueer ghost! You friendly chalk faery and PacMan Ghost. Hello hello. We missed you. Blulip, it's Orsun Ursol, returning in style! Having largely disintegrated into filth on the lino floor, Orsun Ursol had reappeared in Exquisite Corpse incarnation. P.I. Belahg did not know it yet, but this was the beginning of a grand finale on Harpur Street. This was the Monday evening after Saturday's launch of the Deadwood-to-Dynamo Audience Prize. Unsuspectingly, P.I. Belahg and Blulip had been watching TV. They did not know it yet, but Orsun Ursol had not come on her own.

The bell went. It was Pink&Brown Bedsheet Ghost. It was pre-Bikini-Atoll's interpretation of a Pink&Brown Bedsheet Ghost. Pre-Bikini, the 12-year-old from West Croydon, had based their Pink&Brown Bedsheet Ghost on the Orsun-Ursol-like *Cadavre Exquis* broadcast on Tulep.tv. Killing the universalist White Bedsheet Ghost, pre-Bikini's Pink&Brown Bedsheet Ghost was a Deadwood-to-Dymano Audience Prize submission. As Pink&Brown Bedsheet Ghost, Pre-Bikini had come to submit herself in the flesh. Heh, Blulip! We have a forerunner. 12-year-old Pre-Bikini has taken an early lead. Pink&Brown Bedsheet put on an impromptu show. She killed the White Bedsheet Ghost dead. Boo! Gone. Oops, there was universalist White Bedsheet Ghost again. Watch out, Pink&Brown Bedsheet Ghost. It's behind you. Pink&Brown Bedsheet Ghost whirled around, re-annihilating the White Bedsheet Nightmare. They killed, it returned, they killed, it returned.

Kill, return, kill, return, kill return. Kill. It would take the whole evening.

Strong entry, Blulip said.

The bell rang again. What fresh hell?! Who is it now? It was the Transgender Arabesque with her permanent wave gelled back. Hi! What brings you here? The Transgender Arabesque (aka TA) had come in her capacity of guest judge. She declared herself Chair of the Deadwood-to-Dynamo Audience Prize Committee. Actually, she declared herself the benchmark. The Transgender Arabesque declared herself the benchmark against which all D.-t.-D. Audience Prize submissions should be measured. The Transgender Arabesque had come in her capacity of gold standard of dynamic deadwood.

Already the standard of submissions to the inaugural Deadwood-to-Dynamo Audience Prize was high. Pink&Brown Bedsheet Ghost, for example, came up to TA's waist.

"Where's GoldSeXUal?" TA asked. The Transgender Arabesque was looking for the GoldSeXUal StatuEtte. But the GoldSeXUal StatuEtte had yet to return to her former cruising ground. The GoldSeXUal StatuEtte, or Sxuse, has yet to revisit her original cruising ground, Blulip replied. Ah, TA cried, Princess Blulip! Where is your headgear? Put your crown on, go on. It's the Deadwood-to-Dynamo Audience Prize Award Ceremony! Is it?! When, now? Yes. It's the Deadwood-to-Dynamo Audience Prize Award Ceremony and D.-t.-D. Gala. The Transgender Arabesque indicated her glamorous gown (*fig. 3*). "I have my best brogue on," she said. Look. Ok, Blulip said. Blulip resigned herself to wearing her crown during the ongoing Deadwood-to-Dynamo Audience Prize Award Ceremony and D.-t.-D. Gala. But where was it? Where was Princess Blulip's crown? "It's over there," TA said. The Transgender Arabesque pointed at the *Cadavre Exquis,* mugshot of Belua, topsy-turvy tulip, Maxillary Molar, and spitting image of an inverted crown. This isn't my crown, Blulip objected. This is Orsun Ursol's most recent incarnation and the inspiration behind Pink&Brown Bedsheet Ghost. *Ach so*, TA said. P.I. Belahg, could you find my actual crown? Blulip asked. Please, P.I. Belahg? "It might take a while," P.I. Belahg admitted. Belahg, Blulip continued. Did you know it's the Deadwood-to-Dynamo Audience Price Award Ceremony and D.-t.-D. Gala? No. P.I. Belahg had not known the first thing about it. Let's invite Hilary Park and Rocky Bobàk, Blulip said. Belahg, call them? Tell them that Orsun Ursol, Pink&Brown Bedsheet Ghost, and the Transgender Arabesque are already here. Ok. P.I. Belahg rang Hilary Park. "Who's there?" Hilary said. "All the ≈Δ≈," Belahg replied. It's the Deadwood-to-Dynamo Audience Prize Award Ceremony and D.-t.-D. Gala, and riffraff are gathering on Harpur Street. Come? "Ok," Hilary said and hung up.

Tracey Biryukov Lulip was wearing her *Christoper Ala* white/orange shark-print T-shirt and camouflage joggers from *Tesco* for the Deadwood-to-Dynamo Audience Prize Award Ceremony and D.-t.-D. Gala. No crown. P.I. Belahg was wearing her *Beirendonck* skirt and Pegasus print sweater. Now what, the Transgender Arabesque said. Let's pick a winner, Belahg said. We must have a winner. Peggy reared on Belahg's sweater. Peggy, for one, was raring to go. *'On y va!'* ran towards the hem of Belahg's sweater in metallic lettering. Let's go, let's go! 'Let's go' no longer meant 'let's-get-the-hell-out-of-here', but 'let's get going'. P.I. Belahg, Blulip, the Transgender Arabesque, Pink&Brown Bedsheet Ghost, Peggy and hundreds of *Christopher Ala* sharks crowded around the white plastic laptop. Blulip entered her password: BeLAhG <3 <3 <3. Oho! The D.-t.-D. online manager was brimming with submissions, comprising anything from traditional to multi-media formats.

The Deadwood-to-Dynamo criterion stipulated that she who turned Deadestwood into Dynamost should be the winner of the inaugural Deadwood-to-Dynamo Audience Prize. She who turned piss into gold. The D.-t.-D. Committee went through the submissions with the Deadwood-to-Dynamo criterion in mind. Eventually,

P.I. Belahg and Pink&Brown Bedsheet Ghost proposed a shortlist. Blulip and the sharks objected. What, this and not this? Blulip and the sharks opposed P.I. Belahg and Pink&Brown Bedsheet Ghost's proposed shortlist. The decision was made by the self-appointed Chair of the D.-t.-D. Committee

The bell went again. "Tracey Biryukov Lulip, Director General of Tulep.tv?" Yes? It was a satellite from the Arts Council England (ACE). In Socialist Britain, the ACE was pioneering a satellite system. The system was designed actively to locate those who lacked the specific language (Oxford English) to apply and succeed through the conventional channels. It was a proactive equal ops scheme. Kept the welfare bill lower, too. Tulep.tv's trailblazing programming had piqued this satellite's interest. Isn't this Healthy-lips over there? the ACE satellite cried. And aren't they the new UUs? As featured in the *2nd Episode*? Seeing the new UUs off Tulep.tv in the flesh helped loosen this satellite's purse strings.

The doorbell again. It was Channel 4. Channel 4 was not here to follow up on Querbird, nor its previous investment. Forget Querbird. Nor did Channel 4 think that Tulep.tv had a future on national TV. However, Channel 4 did think that the Deadwood-to-Dynamo Audience Prize might be of potential interest to national audiences. In Socialist Britain, Channel 4 was committed to representing inspirational working class initiatives on public-service TV. It responded to public demand for inspirational migrant and QTIPoC (Queer/Trans/Intersex Persons of Colour) representation, 24/7. The D.-t.-D. Audience Prize ethos and idea had legs, Channel 4 said. We would like to invest. Oh great, the ACE satellite said. Channel 4 is investing. The Arts Council England was now in the position to offer their award to Pink&Brown Bedsheet Ghost. Here you go, Pink&Brown. Happy future. Both public bodies left standing order forms (enter your bank details here), then left.

Finally, Hilary Park and Rocket Bazcjk arrived. They were wearing their *Helper Cell* T-shirts and colourful joggers. Hilary was wearing her *Nashir Mazhar* cap with the side pencil holder, and Bazcjk was wearing hair clips in her short boy's hair cut. Hello, Hilary, hello, Bazcjk.

Who won? Hilary cried. Have we missed it? I'm afraid, you just missed the Deadwood-to-Dynamo Award Ceremony, Blulip said. The Chair of the D.-t.-D. Committee TA has announced a winner and runner-up. But the D.-t.-D. Gala continues to rage. Aah, Hilary said, ok. What's with them?! Pink&Brown Bedsheet Ghost sat on their substantial Arts Council England award, crying. They hadn't won. Who won?! Bazcjk reiterated. Winner of the inaugural Deadwood-to-Dynamo Audience Prize was Afafa F. from Bethnal Green, E2, for staging a version of Spartacus on their 20 sq ft balcony with pigeon netting. Runner-up was P.I. Belahg for OperaBo. OperaBo? P.I. Belahg? Runner-up?!

PLATZE, BO!

What was OperaBo? Was OperaBo operatic? Operative? Or what? Let's go back a day or two. The day before yesterday. Let's start with Beau.

P.I. Belahg decided to give the Deadwood-to-Dynamo Audience Prize a go. She fancied her chances. When she started working on her submission, she did not anticipate OperaBo as such. At the beginning, she did not anticipate anything. Remember the aqua-*bleu* budgerigar figurine with the varicose-veined, goose-bumped and otherwise featureless 'hard test' head? The aqua-*bleu* penultimate model that the camera had not loved? P.I. Belahg attempted to film her. But oh dear. Beau was not good on camera. In terms of the D.-t.-D. Audience Prize, P.I. Belahg saw her hopes dwindling. Look at the spoiler. The D.-t.-D. Committee wouldn't give Beau a second look. What now? How to impove her piece? P.I. Belahg was considering her options. That's how Bo came in.

Bo was one of Rocky Bobák's placeBOs. On top of her lipstick reinforcement organs and her *Helper Cell* T, Rocky Bobák had been recruiting oral placebos to aid her convalescence. A placebo is a medically ineffectual substance. But ineffectuals had been running this show, even before P.I. Belahg, Tracey B. Lulip, Hilary Park, and Rocky Bobák had articulated the Deadwood-to-Dynamo principle. Dummies had been looming large at Blulip's on Harpur Street, wheeling and dealing and calling the shots. There were no ineffectual substances around here, only dynamic deadwood. Therein lay P.I. Belahg's cunning. P.I. Belahg was banking on Bo having an effect on Beau. 'Placebo' stands for 'I shall please'. P.I. Belahg put Bo and Beau next to each other, so that Bo might exert a pleasant influence upon Beau.

Nothing, however, so far. Filming Bo next to Beau had not improved Belahg's shot. Ok. Now what.

Placebo became '*Platze*, Bo!'. Remarkably, '*Platze*, Bo!' is

German for 'Bo, Explode!'. '*Platze*' translates as 'Explode'. '*Platze*, Bo' gave P.I. Belahg her idea. First, the creative detective bisected Bo. Bo was a telescope cellulose capsule. P.I. Belahg pulled Bo apart, emptying her, Bo, of her usual content (potato starch). Now there were two cellulose thimbles. P.I. Belahg filled one of the thimbles with a medically inert, but pyrotechnically potent household chemical (potassium nitrate, scraped off the heads of matches). Then she joined the two halves back together, restoring Bo. Finally, P.I. Belahg glued Bo into Beau's face moustache-like. Better. Prettier Beau. Gayer.

Still, not gay enough. P.I. Belahg returned Beau to her regular position. As the penultimate model, aqua-*bleu* Beau's place was next to Healthy-lips. Perhaps Healthy-lips, too, could appear in the video? A fail-safe (?) representation of Tulep, for most of this gig Healthy-lips had been P.I. Belahg's primary investigative lead.

Ultimately, 'OperaBo' did not stand for 'operatic'. 'OperaBo' stood for 'I shall work'. Bo worked. Bo's potassium nitrate content, once lit, produced small pyrotechnic emissions. P.I. Belahg recorded indoor fireworks on her phone. Suddenly, fiery Beau fell like a domino tile, knocking neighbouring Healthy-lips smackbam in the tooth with her forehead. The aqua-*bleu* penultimate model Beau fell sideways, smashing her forehead directly into Heathy-lips's lip. Not that the headbutt affected Healthy-lips's balance. Not that it knocked out her human tooth. Rather, Beau's forehead, on impact, coloured Healthy-lips's tooth aqua-*bleu*. Aqua-*bleu* = turquoise. Bright turquoise stuck to Healthy-lips's Maxillary Bicuspid. Clasping a turquoise pompom in her beak, a real-life budgerigar was galloping across the workbench like a formidable micro-horse. P.I. Belahg did a double take. Turquoise pompom *vis-à-vis* turquoise bicuspid, the real-life budgerigar looked the spitting image of Healthy-lips. They looked identical. All investigatory leads pointed towards the real-life budgerigar. That there was Tulep.

The End

APPENDIX 1

TULEP.TV: THE COMPLETE SERIES

1. The *1st Episode* features chalk/tooth faery Orsun Ursol.
2. The *2nd Episode* showcases the inquisitive transarmy, in the context of the new UUs and Healthy-lips. The battlefield *d'Amour.*
3. The *3rd Episode* features the GoldSeXUal StatuEtte. The GoldSeXUal StatuEtte is a compound character, comprising Hilary Park balancing on the back of the new UU fibreglass cygnet and Blulip wearing a gold crown.
4. The *4th Episode* features the GoldSeXUal StatuEtte encountering the Transgender Arabesque. Two LGBTQI giants are navigating the tiny space of Blulip's council flat/workshop. This is Tulep.tv's breakthrough episode in terms of audience reception and social media traction.
5. The *5th Episode* features Colt, a dead sea urchin, in surreal lighting.
6. The *6th Episode* features Belahg and Blulip as AxoLottl and Painlevé Hypercamp, engaging in hypocamp hanky-panky.
7. The *7th Episode* features Hilary Park and Rocky Bobák framing the *Cadavre Exquis* mugshot. The live broadcast turns into an impromptu call for submissions and the launch of the Deadwood-to-Dynamo Audience Prize.
8. The *8th Episode* is *'Platze, Bo!'*, the Season Finale (forthcoming).

APPENDIX 2

P.I. LOVEDAY'S WALL CHART

Still invested in the idea of a linear plot, P.I. Loveday from Holborn Detectives PLC has been constructing a series of wallcharts. Reprinted below, the wallcharts were designed to help her make sense of Tulep.tv's programme. Arranging all seven existing episodes in various orders, P.I. Loveday come up with four recognisable (classic) narratives and interpretations. "What's wrong with a theme and a plot we can all follow?" (Split Britches, *Belle Reprieve,* 1995) P.I. Loveday has been asking herself the same question.

1, 2, 5, 3, 6, 7, 4:

1. Murder!
2. Murder in Disneyland Paris. They're sending the army into Disneyland Paris. Who's that in the background? The one with the blood-smeared mouth? She must have done it.
5. A dead body floating in Lake Disney.
3. Inspector GoldSeXUal arrives on scene. All will be well.
6. Another stabbing.
7. They issue a BOLO. An ALT.
4. Inspector Transgender Arabesque replaces Inspector GoldSeXUal who fails to press charges against anyone. No conclusion.

1, 3, 4, 2, 7, 5, 6:

1. The lead actor is the one that looks like a PacMan Ghost, or a crown in various positions. There she lies on the floor, relaxing.

3. Now the lead actor is riding on the head of another character. She parades through a populous landscape like a king.
4. More characters enter the scene. This does not affect the lead actor and king. King keeps on riding.
2. A military uprising in the king's populous country. Now that things are getting difficult, the king is nowhere to be seen. The king has disappeared.
7. The king is on the news! Having deserted her country, the king is reported for going AWOL. AWOL is a military term for Absent Without Leave.
5. They recruit a crystal ball. The crystal ball suggests that the king is dead.
6. The king is dead and does not feature in this scene. The king's subjects prosper in the king's absence.

4, 2, 5, 3, 1, 7, 6:

4. They are Mother and Father. Mother is pregnant. She is wearing a maternity dress.
2. They have got a number of children already.
5. They have no money, no gold. They wish they had.
3. But they don't. Father leaves Mother and abandons his children. Here he is, on his own.
1. Mother gives birth to this baby.
7. This is the baby with new adoptive parents.
6. Mother, not pregnant now, gets herself a female lover. She looks much better for it. Entirely different.

2, 3, 4, 5, 6, 7, 1:

2. A universal enigma is posed, such as 'Why are we here?', or 'Why is there something rather than nothing?' . Hoofed Cygnet vows to find the truth.
3. Hoofed Cygnet embarks on her journey, but others are holding her back. They are weighing her down.

4. Fairy Arabesque appears. She tells Hoofed Cygnet to persevere and to look for the truth in unlikely places.
5. Does the truth lie at the bottom of a lake?
6. Is love the truth?
7. Is the truth haunting you, too?
1. The truth is the only thing left now. The truth ate everyone else alive.

ACKNOWLEDGEMENTS

Thanks to the University of Roehampton and the Department of English & Creative Writing for funding *Gaudy Bauble*. Victoria Brown & Richard Brammer at Dostoyevsky Wannabe for publishing *Gaudy Bauble*. Eley Williams & Joanna Walsh (3:AM), Russell Bennetts (Berfrois, Queen Mob's), Allison Grimaldi-Donahue (Queen Mob's), & Fernando Sdrigotti (Minor Literature[s]) for publishing my fictions, you are the future of publishing. Heidi Nam for friendship. Sarah Wood for friendship, Cheam, long-term encouragement, inspiration, & reading *Gaudy Bauble*. Sara Ahmed & Sarah Franklin for friendship, two Clerkenwell Christmasses, one Easter, & their combined libraries. Emma Jackson for friendship. Tahani Nadim & Sophie MacPherson for reading, from the beginning. Irene Revell for gay bars. Verena von Stackelberg, Rachel Anderson, Ros Murray, Nazmia Jamal, Ego Ahaiwe-Sowinski, Ruth Höflich, & Charlotte Prodger for inspiration. Sarah Schulman for reading & commenting on *Gaudy Bauble*. Jeff Hilson, Peter Jaeger, Joanna Zylinska, Gary Hall, & Matt Fuller for reading *Gaudy Bauble*. Damian Owen-Board & Odhran O'Donoghue. Club des Femmes, Electra, & Goldsmiths Centre for Feminist Research for community & inspiration. Goldsmiths Department of Media & Communications, particularly Louise Chambers. Valerie Walkerdine for inspiration, & for giving me a job. The Arts Council England. Families Waidner, Wöhrle, & Alan Cheetham. Olivia Laing for the queer avant-garde. Sarah Wood & Ali Smith, again, for friendship & Che<3m. Excerpts from *Gaudy Bauble* were published in Makhzin: Feminisms (eds. Mirene Arsanios et al., 2016) and Berfrois (2017). *Gaudy Bauble* is dedicated to Lisa Blackman.

ABOUT THE AUTHOR

photo : self

Isabel Waidner is a middle-aged (born 1974) Londoner of Germandescent. She has published ~~[illegible]~~ volumes of fiction ~~and six of non-fiction~~. She ~~is a vegetarian and~~ campaigns ~~for the rights of other-than-human animals as well as for the rights of writers (still widely treated as sub-human). She is an active trade unionist (a member of the Executive of the Writers' Guild of Great Britain) and, with her fellow-writer Maureen Duffy, organised the campaign for British PLR. She is married to Michael Levey, writer, art historian and Director of the National Gallery, and they have a grown-up daughter~~.

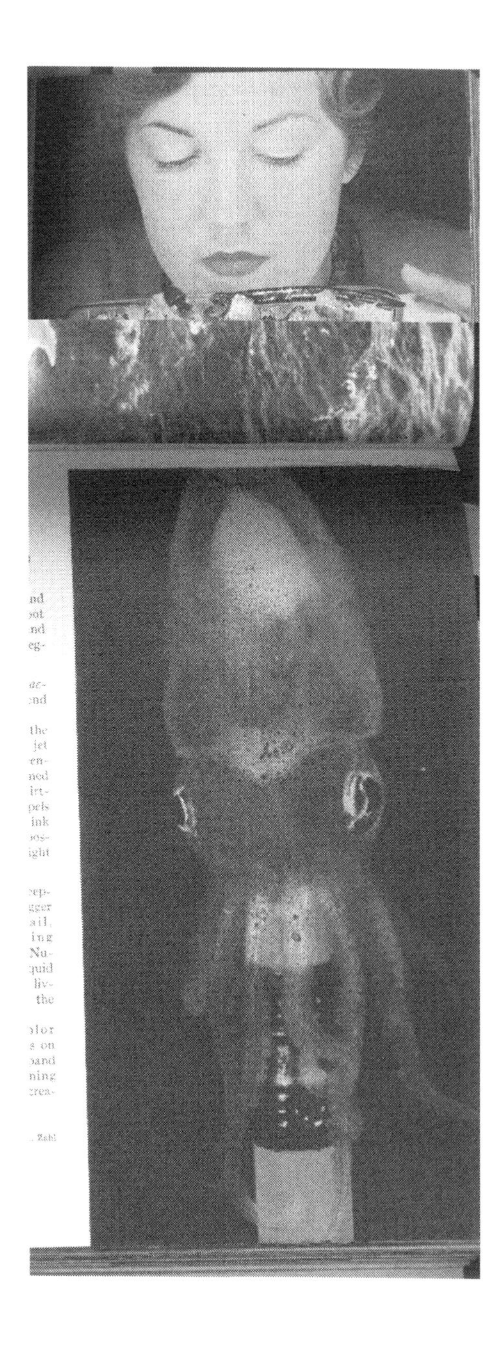

Image by Sarah Wood (for *Gaudy Bauble*)

Dostoyevsky Wannabe Originals
An Imprint of Dostoyevsky Wannabe

Printed in Great Britain
by Amazon